Warfare
Rise Of Mankind Book 2

John Walker

DISCLAIMER

This is a work of fiction. Names, characters, business, places, events, and incidents are either the products of the author's imagination or used in a fictitious manner. Any resemblance to actual persons, living or dead, or actual events is purely coincidental. This story contains explicit language and violence.

Blurb

Barely recovered from a battle against an alien incursion, the Behemoth waits to see how the alliance wishes to leverage their discovery, the weapon code named Protocol Seven. When two warships arrive from their allies with an offer difficult to refuse, they find themselves leant out to travel outside the solar system to a secret research facility across the galaxy.

But what was promised to be a milk run turns into something completely different. With limited resources and a new commander on board their companion ship, they must stay alive. Combined with a potential threat from within, the odds are stacked high against them. Only their ingenuity and the perseverance of the human spirit may keep them alive.

Prologue

Kale Ru'Xin struggled to stand. His ears rang and he blinked his eyes to clear his blurry vision. People shouted around him, some screaming for help and others for direction. He turned to his right and saw the body of Weiz Fi'Dae, his Anthar and mentor for the past three years. The man's lifeless eyes tilted upward, his unmoving chest lay slack.

What happened? How did we get to this? Am I in a battle? Hurt? Dead? The questions flooded his mind but he couldn't find answers. The last thing he remembered involved a signal they investigated on the outskirts of the system then...engagement! The enemy attacked and we engaged.

The violence around him, the carnage, all came from exchanging pulse blasts with an overwhelming force. They didn't come out of nowhere, that trick long since ceased to be effective, but their first strike tactic proved more than effective to get in and cause havoc. No matter how often they came, it still felt wrong that sentient beings could be involved in such horror.

"Su-Anthar!" Kale's rank snapped him out of his reverie and he pushed himself back to his feet. The sounds of the bridge closed around him, the alert blaring against the chatter from the speakers. He leaned against the chair and turned to Maika, a recently appointed ZAnthar who piloted the vessel. "What are your orders?"

Kale directed his attention to the view screen. His squadron was in shambles. The enemy began four ships strong and were down to two, more than a match for Kale and his lone vessel. If he didn't think of something, everyone on board would certainly be dead. He turned to the computer read out and checked the reports of the other ships.

They're dead in the water, he thought, *there's nothing they can do to help but...wait...*

His scans showed no lifeforms aboard and he had to fight back a wave of emotion. All those people, his people...friends and comrades, all gone. A meaningless, stupid attack took so much. He'd be damned if they went down without a real brawl. *You bastards will have to earn your kill today.*

"Maika," Kale said, "full reverse. Put our...our fallen between us and the enemy."

"Sir?" Maika engaged controls but the question hung in the air.

"I have a plan. Do as I say." He turned to his tech Thaina, another ZAnthar who barely left the training grounds. She stared at him with wide, pale green eyes. "Can you tap into the engineering section of that vessel? Link up with their computer?"

"I believe so, sir...to what purpose?"

Kale sat down and took a deep breath. "To save our lives. Weapons officer, lock your pulse blasts on target. Don't fire until I give the word."

"They're firing at us, sir!" Maika shouted. "Evasive!"

"Our shields will hold for another minute," Kale replied, not entirely confident in his statement. "Have you tapped into the computer yet?"

"Aye, sir." His tech replied. "What do you want me to do?"

"Set their pulse drive to overload, five second timer."

"Sir, that will cause a massive...explosion..." Realization washed over Thaina. Kale nodded.

"Then you know what we're up to. Weapons officer, when that explosion goes, it'll rip the enemy shields down. That'll be your chance. I recommend targeting their engineering section."

"Aye, sir. Targets locked."

"Give us a countdown, Thaina."

"Five..." Kale clenched his fists but forced himself to not show any outward signs of stress. It proved difficult. Blowing up that vessel would likely take their own shields with it so this may save them...or seal their fate.

"Four..." Thaina's voice cracked on the number and she stared intently at the controls. Kale wished he could put a hand on her shoulder, or offer any reassurance whatsoever. Discipline, at all costs, his father used to say. The Anthar agreed and constantly preached it. Would he have done the same?

"Three..." A pulse blast shook their ship. Kale saw the shield meter on his console drop to forty percent. The blast that killed his friend and commanding officer slipped right through, a lucky shot hopping the perfect frequency to ignore shields. Luckily, they didn't get another or they'd never have gotten to try this ploy.

"Two…" Kale prepared for impact. When that pulse drive went, it would shake everything around it. The resulting shockwave would fry defensive barriers, essentially sending a cancellation wave into the surrounding barrier.

"One…" Thaina glanced back at him. "Detonation."

The resulting explosion jarred their vessel and filled the view screen with bright, blinding white light. Kale shouted over the rumble, calling out to the weapon's officer, "fire!"

The pulse blasters made the hull shake and another set of explosions resounded off their bow. As the engine cores of the enemy ships detonated, their resulting blast sent Kale's ship veering away from the scene of the battle, tumbling out of control away. Maika fought the controls and after a good two minute fight, stabilized the vessel.

Kale peered into the view screen, holding his breath. Thaina magnified on the debris of their fallen comrades and the four enemy ships now little more than white hot chunks of metal. The others cheered, hugging one another and clapping loudly. Kale slumped in his seat, feeling a sense of relief hit him but as he saw the dead eyes of his friend, he sobered quickly.

A trick, he thought, nothing more. No tactics…just blind luck and better knowledge of my people's technology.

However he did it, most of his crew survived. They, the fortunate ones, could return home and tell the tale. Kale requested his people to scan for survivors while medical teams tallied the casualties. They'd be out there for a while before returning home but he'd offer a partial report over coms shortly.

First, I want to see who survived…then, we can talk about what the other sacrificed themselves for. They deserve an hour or so of our time. This war will continue soon enough. Right now, we honor the fallen.

Kale gave the orders and requested a medical team to come to the bridge. The Anthar needed to be taken out of there, put somewhere respectful so he might return to his family for a proper ceremony. After so many years of service, countless battles and campaigns, a great man died.

Is that the fate of all warriors in these dark times or can I look forward to something different? Something better?

He doubted it. The enemy did not seem ready to give up and his people were no closer to victory. Perhaps they all would share the Anthar's fate someday. Maybe the Gods forsook them. But then, such a victory as what Kale just earned would never happen. He had to have hope, to keep believing.

There's no time for despair. Time to shake this off and make things happen. Good bye, old friend. I won't let you down.

Chapter 1

Gray leaned back in his chair of his office, reading through the various military reports pouring in from other departments. Repairs after the enemy invasion and the arrival of the Tam'Dral went quickly. The hull breach sealed, systems operational, all accomplished in the time frame Higgins promised.

With those out of the way, he could finally focus on the broader picture, what was happening with the refugees and the construction of the next ship which would defend Earth from an additional attack. If they learned anything in the previous battle, it was the absolute necessity to have some backup in a fight.

Engineers started out optimistic, especially with the resources gathered from the destroyed ships. Unfortunately, while the hulls were completed and the ships able to be inhabited, key parts were still required to bring the pulse engines online, parts Earth simply did not have access to.

A debate began on whether or not they should dismantle the Tam'Dral and reverse engineer it. Some claimed Earth owned the ship while others fought to keep the vessel in the hands of the people who brought it. They didn't have a home, after all and their conveyance was the only thing left of their culture.

They'd proven to be quite helpful with both understanding their technology and acclimating to their status as a race seeking asylum. Captain Paltein in particular had high praise for the Behemoth crew. Without his help and that of his ship, the enemy may well have destroyed Earth.

However, the Tam'Dral was not a warship despite it's capabilities. Paltein administered vessels, but never as a military man. Prior to their exodus, he piloted cruise ships meant to give his civilian population tours of their solar system. Study groups visited his old ship and the Tam'Dral proved far more advanced than anything he managed before.

Gray advocated for them keeping the ship and also adding those who were so inclined to join the military. They needed every able body they could get but many felt leery about accepting aliens into the mix. Having Clea on board was one thing, a single foreigner couldn't do much harm but an entire ship full? That went beyond practicality for the conservative minded.

The Tam'Dral remained in Earth orbit under guard and the civilian crew underwent a series of medical exams to ensure they could even survive on the surface. Most of them never encountered a human virus before and vice versa. Such study was insisted upon by the council who wanted to protect the safety of everyone involved.

Gray's own people were torn on the issue. He heard the debates aboard the Behemoth. Some wanted to send the Tam'Dral away and have it head back into Alliance space. "Let them find asylum with those people, they're better equipped for it anyway." Others fought against it, citing the fact that they helped save human lives.

He believed in inclusion rather than isolation. The galaxy proved to be much smaller than anyone anticipated and if any one culture planned to thrive, it needed to acknowledge the others. The enemy they all faced seemed intent on unifying things under fire and blood. Fractured civilizations would fall to them easily.

Unity was their only real chance.

Earth continued to drag its feet on a plan of action. Despite the recent attack, they didn't know what they wanted to do. They liked that Clea contacted the alliance and seemed to hold out hope a ship might arrive soon. Contact with their allies had been sporadic in the years since they intervened in the attack so a meeting would be most welcome.

A knock on his door drew him out of his reverie and he tapped the remote button to open it up. Adam, his first officer, stepped in and offered a salute. "Captain," he said, "do you have a moment to talk?"

"Have a seat." Gray motioned to the chair across from his. "What's on your mind?"

"I just wanted to let you know, we've restocked supplies and ordinance. Those fighters which were not able to be salvaged have been replaced and all repairs are complete. Personnel has also been supplemented and they're acclimating to life on board. We're ready for active duty again whenever you give the word."

Gray smiled. "Thank you for the update but you know it's not my call. I want to be out there, colluding with our allies over Protocol Seven. I'm sure they'll be interested in it. The war effort will be very different if we can just pass it over."

"But it's not safe to send it by drone," Adam added. "They have to come, sir. I'm sure Clea made a passionate plea."

"Trust me, Clea made it sound like the second coming." They chuckled. "In all seriousness, I'm curious what'll happen when our allies arrive. What will the council do? I'm usually good at predicting their behavior but this time...I really don't know."

"We need resources," Adam said. "Our own solar system isn't providing what we need to complete that vessel and without it, without a defensible fleet, we can't withstand another attack. And they've only been sending two at a time! What if they send four? Or ten?"

"I've been thinking the same thing." Gray considered the ADF Nile and the pointless sacrifice they made when trying to help. They died instantly, one attack destroyed them. If the Behemoth didn't get some advanced help, the Earth would remain vulnerable. "We can't settle with one ship either. We'll need more. Two won't cut it. Not if we want to participate in a galactic theater."

"Yes, we need a fleet." Adam sighed. "Our situation is getting frustrating."

"We're making progress, don't worry about that." Gray turned to the reports. "And we've got the Tam'Dral if things get too dire. I'm sure we'd be able to utilize them again if necessary."

"I wish the council would take into consideration that ship's fabrication units." Adam was talking about the factory in the center of the ship which built the drones in record time from recycled parts. Their own engineers examined it but even the Tam'Dral crew had a hard time explaining how it worked. "We could do a lot with that."

"The scientists who built that thing are long gone. It's sad...they were so advanced and yet, their culture...was pretty much ended."

"Just goes to show what we have to look forward to if we don't do something."

"We've done a few things. The Behemoth was a good start. And resources aside, we're not slacking. I think we'll be able to handle more than you know...given the opportunity."

"That's the key though, sir. Our opportunities are slipping because we don't engage with our allies. They abandoned us, plain and simple."

"Now, now, let's not go that far. Clea's here."

"One of their own! And yeah, she's been helpful but imagine what a team of them could've done? Or a few ships for that matter!"

"They're at actual constant war," Gray replied. "They can't afford a few ships. I think they gave us everything they had at their disposal and look at the bright side: they could've just let us die."

"Good point." Adam deflated. "Can you make another petition to join the fight abroad?"

"No, I'm not going to even bring it up. They've made it clear that the Behemoth is the shield of the Earth. I won't push them to replace me because I refuse to accept their order." Gray stood. "Any way, you should enjoy this downtime while you have it. Soon, we might be in a serious situation, a state of conflict which won't allow for rest. Take it while you can, Adam. I insist."

"Sounds like we may not have an option." Adam stood as well. "Thanks for seeing me, sir. I'll see you on the bridge later."

"Remain confident," Gray said as his friend reached the door. "We won another battle. That means we can win more."

"I'll keep that in mind, sir. Good afternoon."

Alone again, Gray peered out the window into space. The vastness overwhelmed his senses, the thought of no relative motion or distance startled him. He never disrespected the vacuum beyond his vessel, the endlessness of distance. His didn't share his awe often but he noticed few of his crew really understood what it meant when someone said out there.

The solar systems beyond their own were not merely the neighbor's backyard but entire worlds, cultures so distant and old they made humanity look like children. The enormity of it should've been too much to contemplate, too much to handle. He appreciated it and as a result, believed himself to be the right man to defend it.

Adam's heart was in the right place. He wanted to protect what he loved and held dear, what he believed in. His convictions were strong and they occasionally got the better of him but he never backed down from a fight, especially where innocent lives were concerned. During the battle, he distinguished himself to be of good character and judgment.

If ever he commanded his own vessel, Gray believed he would do an admirable job.

But his executive officer was right. Something had to happen soon. The enemy could only lose so many ships before they went looking to discover what happened. Eventually, they'd send a larger force, an engagement the Behemoth could not handle. Not with all the tricks up his sleeve nor the perseverance of his valiant crew.

The alliance must know it too. Clea said the transmission had to have arrived with the Protocol Seven information. When they received it, when their council reviewed her comments, they would need to act. The only way Earth would relinquish the technology was in a direct hand off, from one ship to the next.

Security meant the world to them. It was like capturing an enigma box from the Nazis during World War Two. Revealing the information to the enemy may well make it worthless. Gray believed in why they were being cautious but he hoped the gravity of the situation weighed properly with their allies.

The sooner they traded their secrets, the sooner they could finish the war and with Protocol Seven up their sleeves, they finally had the advantage. Time to take advantage of it...before it no longer mattered.

***

Lieutenant Oliver Darnell sat back in his seat, rubbing the back of his neck while sipping from his cup of coffee. No matter how many times he worked second shift, he never seemed to get used to it. Fatigue weighed on his eyes and the only cure involved a good dose of caffeine. By the time he went through his second cup, he felt more like himself.

His scans scoured the solar system, checking in on all their early warning beacons. The process was automated so he just had to sit back and wait for them to pick anything up. They tended to run constantly, pinging for anything out of the ordinary. It's how they encountered the Tam'Dral when it arrived and how they found out about the enemy attack before it happened.

"Adjusting orbit by point three-seven," Lieutenant Commander Stephanie Redding, the senior pilot, announced. "Tim, can you confirm my navs?"

Lieutenant Timothy Collins worked on navigation. He peered at his monitors and performed a series of calculations before nodding. "They look good, Steph."

"Thank you." Redding initiated the change and the thrusters engaged, moving the Behemoth to a more stable orbit. "Next correction in...thirty minutes. Anything on scans worth noting, Olly?"

Olly glanced in her direction. "Nah, it'll let us know if anything comes up. I've programmed it to—"

His console began beeping incessantly.

"Uh oh..." Olly tapped his screen frantically, bringing up the beacon sending back a signal. His heart sank. So fast? Already? Damn, guys, can you give us a breather? "We have contacts."

"How many?" Redding asked. "Are you sure?"

"As sure as I was last time," Olly replied. "Two massive ships incoming...just like last time. Damn it!"

"I'll contact Commander Everly," Redding said. "Just keep up on those scans and get me a silhouette ASAP. I want to know what we're dealing with."

Olly acknowledged, bringing up his various applications to analyze the incoming ships. The last time it happened, the Tam'Dral appeared followed closely by the enemy. God knows what these guys want. A fleeting moment of hope entered his heart—it could be the Alliance come to ask about Protocol Seven.

I really pray that's who just showed up on our doorstep. It feels like we have an open invitation to visit. Hey, fate...can we revoke that already? It's getting a little stressful.

Chapter 2

Clea reclined in her bunk, reading from her tablet. Human literature gave her the best source of education she could hope for. Even spending time amongst them, going about her daily life in their presence didn't offer as much as one of their celebrated authors. She'd gone through a variety of them, from what they considered classics to dramatic works of the twentieth century, all of them showed the species in many different lights.

One of her favorites was Stephen King. He rarely painted people positively, focusing instead on their base sides and playing off the horrors dwelling in their hearts and imaginations. She found these books to have a great deal of truth, mostly because the author cast light on the darkest elements of the subconscious mind.

They also scared her a little and that could be fun too.

Another author she spent a lot of time with was Charles Dickens. His stories of the nineteenth century Earth gave her a good indication of how their history went. Like King, he could write about the fantastic but ultimately, he focused on the nature of people. Some of them made less sense to her than others and they seemed to be exaggerated but perhaps that's how human art got the point across.

She particularly enjoyed the Christmas Carol. Scrooge's plight made sense to her because Kielan family culture suffered a similar problem. Each of them set out, eager to make a name for themselves and bring glory to their name but they rarely remembered to stop and enjoy the simple pleasures of togetherness, to celebrate life and affection.

Human holidays in general gave her endless room to study, especially the American inspired ones. Independence Day and Thanksgiving both intrigued her. The history behind them meant a great deal but they'd changed considerably over the years. All of them revolved around food, some healthy, some not so much and while one carried with it explosions, the other bordered on a shopping season.

History continued to repeat itself in that regard as even years after the consumerist culture gave way to a socialist tendency, people still struggled for fantastic deals on or around the holidays. Kielans did not suffer from a similar bargain hunting mentality. When they celebrated, they spent the time with family. The rarity of them getting together demanded total attention to spending time with their loved ones.

"Alert," Everly's voice boomed throughout the ship, pumped into every room through overhead speakers. "Alert, this is not a drill. We have incoming vessels on Earth trajectory. We are on Ready Thirty. All pilots report to your stations. Repeat, all pilots report to your stations. This is not a drill."

Yes, we got that it's not a drill, Commander. Clea stood and pulled on her uniform jacket, buttoning it up. The enemy certainly did not waste time in returning. She couldn't believe their tenacity. What had humanity done to warrant such dedication to their end? Then again, her own people endured siege from these fiends so it shouldn't have been entirely surprising.

They want what they want and their desires include the end of anything unlike them.

She left her quarters and headed for the bridge, moving aside as people rushed along around her. The ship proved itself in a major way during the last engagement, their test flight resulting in a massive battle. Each and every soldier aboard proved themselves up to the task of handling advanced technology, exactly what the alliance hoped to see before admitting the human race fully into the fold.

Along with Protocol Seven, she included that in her report as well.

On the bridge, Gray and Everly stood next to one another, hovering around Oliver Darnell's station. They peered at his screen as he tapped away, quietly working under the scrutiny of his two commanding officers. Clea took her seat, content to wait for the information rather than crowd the lieutenant. She knew he had enough on his plate without six eyes burning behind him.

"Come on, Olly," Everly urged. "What's taking so long?"

"They're moving quickly, sir but our scans don't bounce back instantly," Olly explained. "I'll have the data compiled any minute, I swear."

"We need to know how seriously to take this threat," Gray said. "Should I be calling the council? Or are these the good guys."

Well, at least they're thinking the same way I am, Clea thought. Chances are good it's my people. The enemy doesn't even know they've been defeated here yet…I hope.

"Captain," Ensign Abigail White spoke up. "We're being hailed."

"That's definitely not the enemy," Stephanie said. "Unless they've come to their senses and are looking to surrender."

"Cut the commentary," Gray said, turning to the communication's officer. "Go ahead and put it on speaker."

"Earth Ship Behemoth, this is the Crystal Font," a young man's voice spoke over the com, succinct and articulate, Clea immediately recognized his tone as one of her own. Inside, she let herself relax but outwardly, she maintained her professional demeanor. "We are on approach to your home planet and request you do not fire upon us. We are with the alliance."

The rest of the humans on the bridge all let out a collective sigh of relief. Gray cleared his throat. "Crystal Font, this is Captain Atwell of the Behemoth. Welcome to Earth space and thank you for coming. I assume this has to do with the discovery of Protocol Seven."

"Allow me to put my Anthar on the line." Anthar equated to the Earth title of Captain. "He may have more he can add about that."

"Are we in range for visual yet?" Gray asked.

"Aye, sir." Olly tapped his keys. "And I've got their silhouettes now. I've confirmed that these are two alliance warships. They're transmitting as friends."

"Put their Anthar on screen." Gray sat in his chair and leaned forward as a young man, much younger than any commander Clea saw before, appeared. His teal eyes sat above a delicate face, pale blue hair topping his head in thick locks. He offered a grim expression as the connection established.

"I am Anthar Kale Ru'Xin of the Alliance Navy. We are here on a diplomatic mission to exchange information and discuss an alteration in the treaty our two people have agreed to. Will you grant permission to orbit your planet?"

"Welcome to Earth, Kale," Gray said. "You're more than welcome to orbit the planet. I'll contact the council and let them know you've arrived. Are you in command of these two vessels?"

"Negative, sir. I am in charge of the Crystal Font. In our military, the junior captain is relegated to routine duties such as establishing communications and gaining authorization for a landing. Please do not take this as an insult. It in no way reflects on how we view the importance of your station or ship."

"No offense taken," Gray replied. "We have Clea An'Tufal on board. Do you have a message for her?"

Clea stood and stepped in front of the view screen. Emotions coiled within her. She hadn't seen any of her people in a very long time. She smiled and lifted her hand, extending a greeting in her own tongue. "I'm pleased to see people from home."

"We have much to discuss, Vinthari An'Tufal. I hope you'll come aboard when we arrive while arrangements are made for the council meeting."

"It would be an honor." Clea bowed her head briefly.

"We will be able to orbit your planet in less than six hours. At that time, we will re-establish communications to finalize arrangements. Crystal Font out."

The screen went dark and Gray turned to Clea. "I bet you're excited."

Clea nodded emphatically. "More than you know, sir."

"It's been a while. I hope they've brought you some news of your family, of home."

"They send it along," Clea replied, "but it's always so stale by the time it comes. I look forward to speaking to them in person...to seeing some of my people again."

"Feel free to spend as much time as you need aboard their ship when they get here," Gray said. "This type of opportunity may not come again for a long time. Best to take advantage of it while you've got it."

"I appreciate that, sir." Clea finally smiled, fighting hard not to cry. Tears blurred her vision for a moment but she blinked them away. "If you don't mind, I'd like to retire to my quarters and prepare."

"Feel free." Gray gestured for the door. "I think we've got things well in hand up here."

"Thank you." Clea paused to give him an appreciative look then hurried off. He was right. This opportunity did not come along often enough and she needed to spend as much time with her own kind as she could. Once they gave them Protocol Seven, they'd likely leave again and she had no idea when she would see them again.

Time to make up for lost time...as quickly as possible. Ah, how time suddenly has such a tender meaning. Like the Christmas Carol. Take advantage of the good while I have it for tomorrow, it may be gone again. I won't make that mistake. I swear it.

***

Gray finished up a quick meeting with the council and arranged for them to gather shortly after the Kielans arrived. Excitement prevailed over the ship. Everyone knew why they were there and whether or not they might defeat the enemy came into question. What would the alliance do with Protocol Seven?

The answer might turn the course of the war and history itself. Gray looked forward to their proposal. Their advances in technology made Earth's look backward prior to the first attack. Now that they had a head start, they were beginning to catch up but it would be a while before his people would be as potent in space, at least without a little help.

Perhaps the Kielans might be able to provide the missing parts they needed to fire up the next vessel. Their technicians certainly knew what they were doing. Perhaps Earth already had all the requirements but didn't know how to properly utilize them. This wouldn't have surprised Gray either considering the complexities of the pulse drives.

He got his dress uniform out and summoned Clea to his quarters. By the time he finished pressing it, she knocked and he let her in.

"Hey there," Gray said without looking up from hanging his outfit. "I hope you plan to attend the council meeting with your folks."

"I do." Clea paced over and took a seat. "I hope they're here for more than taking the Protocol Seven."

"Me too. I'm guessing at something big."

"A fair assessment." Clea folded her arms over her chest. "It would not surprise me if Earth receives a formal invitation to join the alliance. That will mean trade agreements and more assistance than you've received until now. If it comes to pass and you accept, things will change quickly for your people."

"I hope for the better." Gray turned to the mirror. "Sometimes, advancement isn't always positive. Change can happen too fast."

"Yes, but we have to welcome it regardless. We have no choice." Clea came up behind him and peered over his shoulder. "You look worried."

"I'm a little nervous."

Clea frowned. "About what?"

"Joining the alliance means going to war. We've had battles...we've won them but a full on engagement? Adding our guns to theirs will mean we go to a front line and campaigns like that are costly in lives and spirits."

"Tell me about it." Clea moved away. "My people have been enduring what you describe for many years."

"Then I hope if what I'm saying is true, we can wrap this conflict up so we can all get back to something positive. Exploring, developing technology, helping each other...anything but violence. I tell you this, when that enemy is stopped, the last thing anyone's going to be thinking about is firing a weapon."

"You'd be surprised how quickly tempers flare and violence follows," Clea said. "Many cultures may even use the conclusion of one conflict to wrap up grievances directly after. Much like the proposition by your General Patton in World War Two. He wanted to re-arm the German people and attack the Russian allies before they became a problem."

"Yes, but that was a different theater then," Gray said. "Back then, uncertainty reigned. With the advancements in our technologies, resources aren't going to be the problem and so far, the alliance has proven to share our ideologies. We're in a fantastic place to build relationships...not force them.

"As you say." Clea bowed her head. "And I do hope you're right."

Gray grinned. "I am sometimes." His com unit interrupted him. He clicked it on. "Captain Atwell here."

Olly replied. "Captain, your shuttle is prepared for departure to take you to Military Command. Whenever you arrive, they can depart."

"Thanks, Olly. I'm on my way." Gray killed the connection and turned to Clea. "Are you ready to go?"

"My bag is packed if that's what you're asking."

"Then grab it and let's get a move on." Gray picked up his things and headed for the door. "Today we see what we've discovered with the Tam'Dral and how we can use it going forward. I sure hope your people are as wily as they seem. We need some serious cleverness to put this to bed."

***

Clea and Gray took a shuttle to Earth and arrived at the base of operations in Florida just outside of two hours. They were given quarters to change and told that the council would convene after lunch. The delegates arrived before them and were put up in the visitor's housing, a decent set of rooms well away from any essential systems.

After a light meal, Clea made her way to the floor of the council. Tight security took nearly twenty minutes to get through and she saw others without her position take longer. Once inside, she lingered in the hallway, leaning against the wall in anticipation of Gray's arrival or that of her people.

The Ru'Xin name rang a bell for her but she couldn't place the family, not immediately. Her own didn't interact with them directly. Looking into Kale Ru'Xin himself, she found he was incredibly young for the Anthar honor, nearly six years her junior. He must've done something exemplary to dash past through the ranks.

Anthar Mei'Gora, she knew. He was friends with her father though she never met him personally, his exploits were often recounted at family occasions. Lately, the alliance used his diplomatic skills over his combat experience and he trained some of the newest commanders in their military. If they sent him, it was to show they meant business with the humans.

Clea doubted any of the council would see the significance but sometimes, politics involved intangible gestures.

Someone tapped Clea on the shoulder and she turned, staring into the eyes of Kale. He smiled and extended his hand, a different man than when he sat on the bridge of his vessel. "Hello," he said. "It's nice to meet you in person."

"You as well," Clea replied. She shook his hand. "I don't believe our families have ever crossed paths."

Kale shook his head. "I don't either but we have such large extended relations, it's hard to know, right?"

"True..." Clea considered him for a moment. "I have so many questions but I feel like I'd be rude to just dive in."

"I think we're going to have time later. Are you going to visit our ships?"

Clea nodded emphatically. "Most definitely. I can't wait."

"I'm sure you at least have one question which you must know the answer to now." Kale tilted his head.

"Well..." Clea cleared her throat. "I am wondering how you became an Anthar so quickly."

Kales expression melted into one of seriousness, he looked away. "Battlefield promotion for the Anthar part...but Sun-Anthar, I earned properly. War has a way of elevating positions quickly. We have chances to shine we might not otherwise experience during peace time. As a result, I've proven myself many times, up to and including this assignment."

"It seems like a waste of talent then," Clea replied, "to send you and Mei'Gora here? Why not put you back on the lines?"

"I think our crew deserved a break," Kale said. "They went through plenty in our last engagement. Plus, I got the opportunity to be the official Anthar of my ship. A simple task felt like just the thing to get acclimated with the crew."

"Do you want to talk about the fight that got you promoted?"

Kale considered the question and shook his head. "Another time, perhaps. Over a drink."

"Fair enough." Others poured into the room around them and Clea shook his hand again. "It was very nice to meet you, Kale. I look forward to a more extensive conversation later."

"To you as well, Vinthari."

Gray approached from behind. "Who was that?"

"The Anthar of one of the two ships," Clea explained. "Very young for the job but seemingly quite capable."

"Yeah? I'm not great at guessing age with you folks but I agree, he sure seems youthful to be a captain."

"They can't all be old men like you," Clea teased.

"Hey, stow that old thing. I'm in my prime." Gray escorted her to their seats. "So here we go. Time to find out what all the fuss is about."

"And hope we're all here to end it." Clea took a deep breath and directed her attention to the council. Anthar Mei'Gora and Kale stepped up to a podium at the center of the room. The older of the two had jet black hair and striking purple eyes. His lean body filled out his dress uniform well, proving he remained in fantastic shape.

The council entered shortly after, taking up their positions in the crescent moon of their table. They weren't big on ceremony thankfully and sat quickly before the Chief of Military Operations, Daniel Burke, addressed those present. He was in his sixties with gray hair and a hard face won from years of military service. Clea only met him once before and thought him wise if a bit cynical.

"Greetings," Daniel spoke with a voice far more robust and powerful than his aged visage would lead one to believe. His command authority remained firmly in place. "We have come together in this emergency meeting to address the arrival of the alliance representatives. It is our hope you have come to engage in a free exchange of ideas. Our information for yours."

Anthar Mei'Gora replied, "Thank you, Chief Burke. We appreciate you allowing us this audience on such short notice. We received Vinthari An'Tufal's message concerning your discovery of a weapon to be used against the enemy. We also understand it has seen a successful test. We wish to learn more about this and discuss what can be done for the refugees from the Xan-Wei star system."

"The people of the Tam'Dral are currently residing in their own vessel," Daniel said. "They've been medically checked but we're taking extra precautions so we don't exchange any diseases either side cannot face. As far as Protocol Seven, we will freely grant you access to the information. We would, however, appreciate a few things in return."

"What are your terms?" Mei'Gora tilted his head up, a sign Clea knew meant he did not appreciate the way Daniel spoke to him. She briefed the Earth council on how to speak to her people. She had no idea why they didn't listen. Instead of mentioning their own demands, they should've allowed the Kielans to offer.

We're generous people. Look at what we've already given you for nothing?

"We are currently building a second vessel, another defender for our solar system but lack the resources to complete the task. Can you assist?"

"Yes." Mei'Gora nodded once. "What else?"

"We need to know how you plan to use the Protocol Seven and what we can do to implement your plans into our own defensive matrices. This technology has proven very powerful and if we're not admitted fully into the alliance, we may well not have any choice but to start weathering frequent assaults on our own."

"My government has extended me the authority to invite your culture to join our alliance," Mei'Gora said. Gray put his hand on Clea's forearm and squeezed it. "Conditionally."

"Oh?" Daniel tilted his head. "Do explain."

"After an initial assessment to determine the viability of using Protocol Seven at all, we will be taking it to a secret facility on the outskirts of our space, a place where we can replicate and perfect this weapon. If you truly wish to join the alliance, it's time we see what you can do. We ask that you send the Behemoth with our ship, escort your technology and see for yourself what our advanced technology can do."

The other council members began speaking all at once and Daniel hushed them. "I'm sure you realize we cannot do that. We would be relinquishing our only defense just to escort technology."

"My second, Anthar Ru'Xin will be taking Protocol Seven to our planet. My ship will remain behind to assist you with the construction of your own vessel and we'll also address your refugee situation. I trust you've done your research on me and know I will be more than capable of keeping this system safe from another breach."

Gray looked at Clea with wide eyes. She shrugged. This surprised her but it meant good things. For one, the alliance was offering admission into their ranks. Free exchange of ideas and trade was close now. One last hoop, a simple mission to a weapon's facility. Those were some of the safest places in alliance space.

Totally hidden and off the grid, the enemy never found one before. They'd be there and back before they knew it. The value went far beyond just seeing another part of space. It meant a collusion of ideas culminating in the prolonged safety of Earth and the eventual destruction of their mutual enemy.

Clea hoped the humans were smart enough to agree.

"Give us a moment to deliberate." Daniel turned to Gray. "Captain Atwell, will you please join us?"

Gray glanced at Clea, "wish me luck". He stepped away, leaving her to sit stiff and nervous. Depending on how the council voted, she, and the Behemoth, would leave Earth space. It had been years since she'd done so. Her heart raced even as she maintained a placid expression. Even a milk run sounded exciting to her, anything to get out and about, to see other systems.

This opportunity for motion seemed too good to pass up. She hoped the council saw it the same way.

***

Gray approached the gathered assembly who whispered in hushed voices. He folded his arms over his chest and waited for them to address him. On the surface, it sounded like they agreed the Behemoth needed to go with the Kielans. He wondered what was left for them to debate.

"Hold on," Daniel lifted his hand. "What do you think, Gray? You've been spending a lot of time with the alien. Do you believe them?"

Clea devoted years of her life to helping humanity and the top brass still considered her the alien. He gritted his teeth for a moment to avoid saying something, then cleared his throat. "Yes, I trust them completely. Clea has proven to be nothing short of a miracle worker and she's put our safety before her own many times, hell...she put our culture before her own by coming here. They're the good guys, sir."

Daniel nodded. "And do you feel your crew is up to the task?"

"If the facility is as secluded as they say, of course. It'll be a cakewalk." Gray frowned. "But my experience tells me nothing is as easy as someone makes it sound. Even so, if we encounter resistance with one of their own ships, then we can take the opposition. These guys have a lot more experience fighting the opponents than we do. I'd love some pointers."

Another council member spoke up, a new one Gray hadn't met yet. Her gray hair was bound up in a tight bun and her craggy face spoke of a hard life. "We'll leverage their technical expertise to finish our own vessel and if they truly want to take the Tam'Dral's woes off our plate, I'd let them."

"Anyone against this?" Daniel asked the others. Marshall Jameson spoke up.

"Yes, I have a big problem with sending our defending ship, the one we control off to some...other solar system for six weeks! God knows how far it is or how long they'll be gone." Jameson shook his head. "This isn't something we want to do."

"How're we going to finish the other ship then?" Marquel stepped in. "They've helped us before and I sincerely doubt they'd come back here to make demands or not follow through on promises. Hell, they're the reason we're still alive. It seems pretty disingenuous if we snub them now."

Jameson waved his hand. "They dropped off a single alien and some tech specs. The rest we handled ourselves. They've practically done nothing for us at all."

"You can't argue that their assistance was instrumental in getting the Behemoth combat ready again," Gray said. "Their pulse technology alone made a huge difference."

"You're rather sympathetic for a mysterious race, Captain." Jameson scowled. "You don't know what they're capable of. When you're gone, they may decide we're a valuable resource, our planet could be strip mined or perhaps something might come up, an emergency pulling them away. We'd be defenseless."

"Don't make this about Gray," Daniel said. "We gave him command of the Behemoth because he's got an open mind, we're not going to give him a hard time about it now."

"Besides, you're being a fatalist," Marquel added. "We've never once received a hint that the alliance would treat us in such a way. They've been nothing but generous. Why would they suddenly, out of the blue, decide to betray us like that?"

Elizabeth cleared her throat, finally contributing to the conversation, "ultimately, we have to weigh the pros and cons here. On the positive side, we gain the tech we need and help with the Tam'Dral. Those folks are in pretty serious need and let's be honest, we're not in a position to do it. Also, admittance into the alliance will work to our advantage."

"And the cons?" Daniel asked.

"We have to trust them." Elizabeth shrugged. "And I can honestly see why Jameson has a hard time with that. We've seen good will, yes but this is something else. Why not send them alone with the technology? Give it to their ships and we'll wait here for them to come back with whatever they discover."

"Our technicians might be instrumental in helping to unlock it's full potential," Gray said.

"Come now!" Jameson scowled. "They built pulse drives for God's sake. I'm sure they will be more than capable of uncovering whatever can be found about this Protocol Seven."

"I don't know," Daniel said. "I'm with Gray for a different reason. I want in on that technology. I want to know we have the advantage immediately. If they don't choose to come back with what they learn..."

"Then we'll simply research it on our own," Jameson replied.

"That hasn't worked so well for our current situation," Elizabeth added. "We are stuck on our second vessel. Our ships have scoured our own system. If I might offer another pro to this discussion, trade would be a very good thing."

"Do you have an opinion one way or another?" Jameson asked. "You're waffling."

"You sound prejudiced to me, Jameson," Marquel added. "Is that what I'm hearing?"

"How dare you!"

Daniel waved his hand. "Enough of that. We're on the same side here!"

Gray spoke up, "you all make excellent points but I'm going to add one more. Those two ships out there are highly advanced, even more so than our own. They may not be able to take as much punishment but they've got technology far beyond anything we've seen. Two of their ships saved us years ago and now, we have the chance to partner with them...not be subservient. They're asking for a partnership, not indentured servitude."

"I agree." Marquel nodded.

"Taking a stance from the financial side," Elizabeth said, "I believe we should agree to help. Send the Behemoth on this run and we will leverage the remaining ship to our advantage. Open trade can begin and as a full member of the alliance, humanity will prosper."

"I'm strongly against this," Jameson said. "The risks are too great, the situation dangerous and all around, this feels wrong. Mark my words, if you go against me on this, we're going to feel it."

"You're a coward," Marquel muttered. "And that type of talk is precisely why humanity remains in the shadows. That isolationist mentality from World War Two and the same prejudice to go along with it."

"Again, that's enough." Daniel sighed. "Anyone else have an opinion?"

They remained silent.

"Alright, and you're sure you're on board, Gray?"

Gray nodded. "Absolutely, sir. We can do this."

"Very well," Daniel said, "Please return to your seat."

Gray joined Clea again as the council stepped back up to their table. None of them sat. Daniel spoke into the microphone. "Anthar Mei'Gora, I have some questions, precautionary if you don't mind."

Mei'Gora nodded. "Please ask."

"What assurance do we have that your ship will stay until the Behemoth returns? You'll be our only defense and we're worried about the lack of Earth oversight."

"Other than my word, I'm not sure what would assure you. I've said it and mean it. Your liaison can explain what it means to us when we make a vow but I'm not sure how you'd believe her if you don't believe me. Suffice to say, we are here to protect you and begin a partnership."

Jameson stirred in his seat.

"Perhaps if you showed us the treaty to join the alliance, we could take that as an act of good faith," Daniel replied. "Even though we won't be signing until the mission completes."

"As you wish." Mei'Gora motioned and his aid approached with a data pad. He handed it to Daniel who clicked it on and read through whatever displayed on the screen. Once he finished, he gave it to Elizabeth. The entire council spent a moment with it, all agreeing except for Jameson who remained stubborn.

"This appears to be in order, Anthar Mei'Gora. We will accept your generous offer. The Behemoth will accompany your ship to the facility. Yours may remain and assist us with our own preparations and any assistance you can provide the Tam'Dral will be appreciated."

Mei'Gora bowed his head. "Thank you, Chief Burke. We look forward to collaborating now and in the future. Arrangements will need to be made, provisioning for a hyperspace voyage and an extended stay at our research facility."

"Very good." Daniel nodded once and turned to the others. "This meeting's adjourned. Section heads, please prepare meetings with your people and the Kielans. These preparations are going to require coordination. Let's not delay because our schedules are already full." He motioned at Gray. "Captain Atwell will prepare the Behemoth for departure. Let's get to work people. We've got a lot to do and I don't want it taking longer than it has to."

Chapter 3

Preparations for departure took five days. Gray met with Mei'Gora for several hours during that time and really had the opportunity to quiz him about engagements near their core worlds. The fighting out there turned out to be far more intense than he ever realized. The enemy lost plenty of ships but they always seemed to have more.

They discussed tactics and theoretical methods to end the war. Gray asked about the enemy's manufacturing capabilities but Mei'Gora knew little. Even when they made initial contact with that culture, they did not ascertain their technological levels. Only when their ideologies crossed violently did the enemy tip their hand.

The Behemoth's database was updated to include newer silhouettes of ships and their technical data. They also received a vast library of star maps, systems well beyond their solar system spanning thousands of light years away. The tech teams were beside themselves and Olly updated all of his apps to account for the new data.

Provisioning took the longest. Supplies came aboard for two days straight and hangar crews started getting surly. Luckily, they'd have two full days of shore leave to relax before they departed. Food wasn't the only thing they received but spare parts and additional fighters to pad their ranks.

Gray put in a request to prepare for war and the council didn't hesitate to agree, much to his surprise. They gave him whatever he needed to be successful, even if the promise involved a relatively short trip.

Adam expressed his own excitement about getting out of there. He believed there'd be a conflict out there. "This is not a simple delivery mission," he claimed. "I feel it."

"I hope your feeling is wrong but if it's not, we'll be ready."

A quick crew survey showed they were torn over the journey. Some expressed excitement, others reservation and a rare few flat out thought the trip was a bad idea. Gray planned to address them all before they left for shore leave, to put some minds at ease and bolster the confidence of those already on board.

Some of the negative comments suggested they should be staying near Earth as defenders, not aggressors. They weren't afraid of combat, but didn't want to do it far from home. Those who felt the opposite suggested a battlefield in the other guy's yard always beat fighting in your own. "Let them deal with collateral damage" became the catch phrase for those behind the journey.

Ultimately, they'd all come around. They knew what they signed up for but some of them probably never thought the day would come. After the last battle, Gray didn't know how anyone could think Earth would last in a purely defensive position. Reactionary conflict never favored the defender.

Clea helped prepare the ship for the first day then planned to spend the last four aboard one of the Kielan ships. He offered to let her go right way but she insisted she spend some time working with the bridge crew. Olly's tech people sure welcomed her assistance. She provided a much needed liaison with her people's experts as they analyzed Protocol Seven.

They quickly agreed that it was definitely the real thing.

Mei'Gora visited the Tam'Dral and agreed to take the people into the alliance. They began plotting which world would be best for them and how they would get there. The people willingly suggested they'd give up their vessel for the fighting cause but none of them were soldiers. They didn't want to participate in the conflict, especially since they were the very last of their species.

Gray wondered who would claim the ship but ultimately, that would be between the council and the alliance to work out. Mei'Gora sure seemed able to make decisions on behalf of the entire alliance though so he suspected they'd figure it out long before the Behemoth returned home.

Just before turning the crew loose on shore leave, Gray initiated a ship wide com on the bridge.

"This is the captain speaking. I know you're all itching to get off the ship and take some much needed rest for the last few days as we scramble to prepare for a deep space voyage. Know that I'm proud of each and every one of you for your dedication and hard work. This historic trip goes beyond anything humanity has ever done. We are pioneers, venturing forth into the unknown.

Some of you have your doubts about the necessity of this mission or the war in general. You wonder if we should even be involved. I tell you we are involved up to our necks. The enemy has attacked us not once, but twice and if given half a chance, they will do it again. Through sheer repetition alone, they may eventually emerge victorious.

I for one will not allow that to happen. For as long as I draw breath, I will fight. Not only to protect humanity from an outside threat but to side with our friends, those who would come to our aid without request or personal benefit. They have earned my respect and continue to do so with every encounter we have.

Each of you is an expert at multiple jobs, professionals and soldiers. Together, we will make history for Earth, for humanity and for the Behemoth. Today marks a time for us to catch our breath before the next sprint and when we start it, you'll have the chance to show the universe who you really are: representatives of our people, stalwart survivors and stubborn combatants.

Enjoy your time off, ladies and gentlemen. You've earned it."

Gray returned home, spending time in the quiet of the country with his books and little technology. Two days of peace worked out well and when he returned to the Behemoth, he felt rested and ready to go. Some of the others spent their time a little less wisely and seemed exhausted from partying but no one showed up late to their duties.

At seventeen-hundred hours, the Behemoth and the Crystal Font linked up their communications and prepared for departure. Ensign Agatha White put them on speaker and Gray addressed the Anthar directly.

"Anthar Ru'Xin, we are showing the green light for departure, do you concur?"

"Captain Atwell," Kale replied, "we are prepared. Our pulse engines are hot and we've plotted a course for a place to perform an optimal hyperjump. We're sending them now. Follow our lead and we should be there inside of seven hours."

"Behemoth confirms." Gray turned to Timothy. "You got them?"

Tim nodded. "Aye, sir. Course plotted and ready. She's all yours, Redding."

"Okay, Crystal Font," Gray said. "Let's move out."

As the engines fired up, the ship pulled out of orbit, moving alongside the Alliance ship. Gray stood and watched the view screen, hands clasped behind his back. Clea also stood nearby, far more tense than he'd seen her before. She fidgeted, which was uncharacteristic. Once they cleared Earth space and headed for the coordinates, somewhere away from any of the planets in the solar system, he turned to Adam.

"Commander Everly, you've got the bridge."

"Yes, sir."

"Vinthari An'Tufal, will you please come to my office?" Gray left the bridge and Clea followed close behind. Neither said a word before they were in private and Gray perched on his desk, gesturing to a chair. "Okay, what's going on?"

"Sir?" She sat down. "I'm not sure what you mean."

"I've known you long enough to recognize when you've got a problem," he said. "You seem nervous...or something. So confide in me. What's up?"

"It's nothing to be concerned with. It won't affect my performance on the ship."

"I'm not sure I agree," Gray replied. "But you can put my mind at ease. Come on, Clea. We're friends...and friends talk."

Clea sighed, averting her gaze to the floor. "I spent time aboard the Crystal Font for the last several days."

"Was it nice to be amongst other Kielans?"

"Yes, absolutely...no regrets there at all but...well...I learned a bit about where we're going. And the Anthar of the Font."

"And those things worry you?"

"Anthar Ru'Xin is a stunning officer. I can't believe he advanced in the ranks so quickly. He's my junior in age and is...was my senior in rank."

"Wait, was?"

"When we finish this mission, I've been promised a promotion," Clea replied. "A new rank in the Kielan military for liaisons. Apparently, there are enough of us now to warrant such an honor. I'll be known as Tathin, which would be the equivalent of Anthar without the responsibilities of running a ship. It will offer me operational priority over the standard military rank for purposes of cooperation."

"Congratulations."

"I'm not sure I take it as a benefit. The responsibility frightens me in one regard. I don't have as much experience as the typical Anthar. I'll be relying heavily upon their advice. In any event, that's not why I'm nervous now. Anthar Ru'Xin got this assignment because his was the only surviving ship in a major skirmish out on the borders. It was a brutal fight and I'm not sure he was ready for active duty."

"That's probably why they gave him this easy assignment," Gray pointed out.

"If it proves to be easy," Clea said. "I'm not sure it will be. However, I hope he's up to the challenge. He seems like a good man and I found him to be delightful but...he has moments of darkness. Whatever he saw in that fight has impacted him."

"War changes people." Gray moved around and sat in his own chair. "I'm sure he'll come out the other side. Is that your only concern? The Anthar of the other vessel?"

"I...learned something about the system we're going to. The research facility. You see, not all of my family joined the military. Some...well, they're scientists."

"I had no idea. I thought family traditions stuck to all members."

"In most cases, yes but those without the physical aptitude to excel in the military find other ways to serve. They still work with the armed forces but in the research capacity. In this case, my sister is one of the lead researchers we are taking Protocol Seven to. Apparently, she's been building weapons for the last year there. I had no idea...it was not in the last letter from home."

"So you're going to get to see your sister." Gray shrugged. "I fail to see how that's a bad thing."

"She's my older sibling. I hope she's not...too harsh on me for what I've done. I believe I'm serving the family well, doing something new but she always stood as my harshest critic. Much as I wish to see a relative, I don't feel up to conflict with one."

"You're an exemplary military officer," Gray said. "You don't have anything to worry about. Remember this, those who criticize loudest are the most insecure. If she says anything against you, it'll be because she knows her own short comings are prominent. Do your best to let it roll off your back. You don't have to prove anything. Your record speaks for itself."

"I appreciate your vote of confidence and it means a lot." Clea shook her head. "I just want them to be happy both with me and for me. I suppose everyone wants the approval of their loved ones, right?"

"Traditionally." Gray smiled. "But you can't please everyone all the time. If you try, you're just asking for trouble."

"I'll try to remember that as well." Clea motioned for the door. "Shouldn't we get back to duty? My personal concerns are keeping the captain from the bridge."

"Adam's got it," Gray replied. "Besides, I'm glad you had the chance to talk about this stuff. Bottling it up wouldn't have helped. You feel better, right?"

"I feel…justified. Better would be a stretch."

Gray laughed. "It's a start, Clea, one I'll accept for now. Come on, before you start to think I'm soft."

"You are," Clea replied. "Otherwise, you would beat me in chess more often."

"Ouch, kindness makes me lose, huh? I'll keep that in mind for the future. For now, let's leave this solar system. That's an adventure all unto itself."

"One I hope you'll never forget," Clea said.

"Me too, Clea. Me too."

Chapter 4

"Commander Everly," Redding spoke up. "We have reached the coordinates for the hyper jump. We're beginning the countdown."

"Very good." Adam tapped his communicator and dialed in the captain. "We're about to perform the hyper jump."

"On my way." Gray's voice crackled on the speakers and faded out. He arrived a few moments later and took his seat. Clea sat beside him on the left, Adam on the right. "So...what should we expect? Two ships jumping at the same time...how do we avoid knocking into one another?"

"Our navigation consoles are synched," Clea replied. "When the Crystal Font begins their countdown, our system will do the same. Much like the enemy's approach during their first attack on your planet, we'll appear in the new system together. I've checked the coordinates and we'll be cutting it close, coming in near the research facility."

"How close?" Adam asked. "Sounds dangerous."

"Thirty minutes away at most," Clea said. "Kielan navigation is tuned enough to make such a leap. The planet's gravitational pull will mask our arrival. If the enemy has long range scans scouring the outer systems, they will not catch the anomaly of our arrival."

"Nice..." Adam nodded. "But still sounds dangerous. If their calculations are off even a little bit, that thirty minutes turns into instant death as we appear in the planet."

"Believe me," Clea said, "our calculations will be fine."

Olly piped in, "I've checked the math several times, sir. It looks perfect."

"Ten seconds," Redding announced. "Crystal Font reports all systems are nominal on their end. We are ready."

"How long will this jump take?" Gray asked Clea. "Our little hop can't be a good indication of time."

"Time will have no meaning," Clea explained. "Much like anesthesia, we will simply find ourselves at the destination."

"Creepy," Tim muttered.

"Stop it." Redding took a deep breath. "Three seconds."

Adam gripped his chair tightly. Here we go, he thought. This is the real test.

The lights flashed once. The engine whined, shaking the hull then, just as it seemed to reach a crescendo, it stopped. Lights burst over head, making Adam wince with the suddenness of their return. Tim coughed and Olly immediately started tapping away at his console, ever the constant worker.

"Report." Gray's voice seemed strained and choked. He rubbed his forehead. Adam tried to stand up but couldn't find the strength. He remained in place, actively trying to recover.

"Coordinates are correct," Olly said. "But...wait a moment..."

"Crystal Font is hailing," Agatha announced. "Emergency frequency."

"On speaker," Adam said.

"Behemoth, this is the Crystal Font." Adam wasn't sure who was speaking...their communication officer perhaps? "Battle stations! I repeat, beat to quarters."

"Get the view screen up," Adam ordered. "What's going on out there?"

The screen lit up, revealing pure chaos. Two other Alliance vessels battled six familiar, hostile silhouettes. Fire erupted from ships on both sides as each blasted away at one another. Gray stood, shouting as he did, "full shields, launch all fighters and fast power the pulse cannons! Get on it, people. Now!"

The crew went into motion. Adam brought Group Commander Estaban Revente on com, ordering the fighters to launch. They didn't anticipate such an engagement directly out of hyper jump so it would take time for them to launch, time they did not necessarily have. The pulse cannons would have to keep the enemy busy along with the Crystal Font.

Surely, four of us can take these guys down but I didn't think they came in such force. Six ships? What are they doing?

"I had the pilots on standby," Revente said. "They'll be out in less than five minutes."

"God bless you for being prepared," Adam said, reporting the news to the captain.

"Excellent." Gray nodded. "How's the Crystal Font?"

"They've powered up weapons and are moving to engage," Olly answered. "The enemy has scanned us but so far, none have disengaged to meet us."

"We're too far to matter," Clea said. She stood. "We need to push it if we're going to help those alliance ships. They're being obliterated!"

"Full power to the engines," Gray said. "Drop the speed when the fighters are ready to launch. We'll come in tight and give them a broadside."

Redding tapped the controls. The engines powered up, humming throughout the ship as they accelerated. Adam joined Gray, leaning close.

"We should use the Protocol Seven," he said. "It'll surprise them...we might not have time to save those other ships if we don't."

"We're already a surprise," Gray replied. "They had no idea we were coming."

"Six on four aren't even odds," Adam pressed. "If we don't use everything at our disposal, we won't win this."

"What's that?" Gray pointed at the screen, gesturing at the planet. "Do you see those flashes?"

"On it." Olly read something before answering. "It seems the enemy has landed a fairly large contingency of troops. They're in the midst of a nasty battle with planetary defense forces. Man, they're shelling each other!"

"I need to speak to Anthar Ru'Xin," Gray said. "Get him on the line."

Kale appeared on the screen. "Captain," he said. "It seems our simple mission has taken a turn for the complicated."

"They've got troops on the planet," Gray replied. "That sounds like they want something to me."

"Indeed, I suspect they intend to take our research." Kale frowned. "We won't make short work of these battleships but we must extract our scientists. If we cannot save the data, it must be destroyed. Whatever happens, the enemy cannot take that facility."

"We can shell it," Adam announced. "Pulverize it from orbit."

Clea stood in a rush, her face flush with uncharacteristic passion. "And murder all those people?"

"Denying the enemy that research is the most important thing, isn't it?" Adam asked.

"No," Clea replied firmly. "No, it is not. Captain, I will personally lead a strike force to the surface to get the data, and the people, out of there. Just give me the word and we'll prepare right now."

"A small force isn't going to help down there." Adam gestured to the planet. "There's no way."

"That's precisely what we need," Clea snapped. "We can get there undetected, download any data we can, destroy what we can't and leave with the personnel." She touched Gray's arm. "Please, sir. We have to try."

Gray looked at Adam who shook his head. There's no way it will work. We're going to throw lives away if we do it. He chose not to voice his concern. The captain would see reason. Dupont wouldn't go for it either and he had say over any ground actions. They had enough problems with the ships in space, they didn't need to add marines into the mix.

"Contact Dupont," Gray said to Clea. "Get a team together and depart as soon as you can. We can't afford any delay."

"Thank you, sir." Clea nodded once and rushed for the door, vanishing down the hall.

"Captain..." Adam shook his head. "That's a mistake."

"We've got some pretty amazing soldiers on board," Gray replied. "I think I'll trust them and try to save some lives before blowing the place up. Besides, we can always rain hell down on the location later. That data has a lot of value and those people know too much to throw away. Have some faith and let's focus on what we're about to get involved in."

"We're just about in range," Olly said. "Fighters are reporting launch readiness in less than a minute."

"Start slowing us down, Redding." Gray moved back to his seat. "Get us turned. I want a full broadside just before the fighters launch. Adam, continue to coordinate with Revente."

***

Gray watched his first officer sit stiffly. He knew Adam didn't like his approach to the planet but destroying the research facility should be a last resort, not the first. Clea's passion aside, attempting to infiltrate the base made sense. When they finished the enemy above, they could lay fire upon the invading force.

"Anthar Ru'Xin, why didn't the invading force drop directly on the facility," Gray asked. "It seems odd to me they'd enter an open battle."

"One of the technologies at work," Kale said. "They must be masking the signature of the base, forcing the enemy to search. That works to our advantage and buys us time. But the battle is upon us!"

"We have range," Redding stated. "Permission to open fire."

"Fire at will," Gray said. "After the volley, launch the fighters. Olly, prepare the Protocol Seven. I think we need to make short work of these bastards to save the facility."

***

Wing Commander Meagan Pointer ran alongside Squadron Leader Mick Tauran. They'd been on standby, waiting near the hangar for a quick launch. Since they did not have the Ready Thirty order, they didn't board their ships but Revente kept them nearby, just in case. Apparently, his paranoia paid off.

"You ready for this?" Mick asked. "Seems crazy we should have to throw down this fast after leaving the solar system. Hell, we didn't even have the chance to look around and be awed by it all."

Meagan grinned. "Nothing surprises me anymore, especially when it comes to Revente's gut feelings. He's survived things no one deserved to because he listened to his instincts. This time's no different."

They nearly collided with Wing Commander Rudy Hale, head of one of the bomber wings. He was a huge man, just shy of too large for regular fighters, he embodied the look for one of the tough, larger vessels.

"Lord, Hale," Meagan complained as she moved around him. "You're like a moving wall or something. You coming on this mission?"

"Yeah, capital ships mean pulse bombs," Rudy replied. "If they use that fancy tech we picked up, we'll tear em up quick. This will be our first chance to see how the rest of this war's gonna go."

"Don't get cocky," Mick said. "This is a whole new game out here."

"We'll see." Hale grinned at them. "See you out there."

"Yeah, just stay out of our way with your slow boats," Meagan shouted back. "Let's make this happen."

The other members of Panther wing, her squadron, boarded their ships and began hastily running through preflight check lists. Meagan brought them up on coms. "I'm not going to waste your time with a long winded speech, guys. This is the real deal, bigger than before. We've got six caps out there and God knows how many fighters.

"Remember to keep your IFFs hot and pulsing because there are friendlies that don't know who the hell we are. I don't want anyone getting shot down over a misunderstanding. Lieutenant Tullefson, welcome to the unit. I wish you would've had a little more time to acclimate to the team but I guess nothing beats a crucible.

"Let's get out there and take down some bad guys."

Meagan's ship throttled up and as the inertial dampeners kicked in, she felt the cockpit pressurize. The tower cleared for launch in ten seconds, just after the Behemoth's first broadside to one of the enemy ships. She felt her heart race with adrenalized anticipation and counted down the seconds impatiently in her head...

***

Gray watched as Redding laid full into one of the enemy vessels, pounding them with pulse cannon fire. Their shields flickered and visible damage across their hull registered. Olly called out, "direct hit!" then began his assessment of what that meant to the enemy. Regardless of how hurt they were, it sure got their attention.

"They won't ignore us now," Gray said, turning to his tablet. The Crystal Font moved in on a different target and a flurry of strange looking pulse beams lit up the sky. They appeared jagged, with purple flickers all along the blue lines. He wished Clea had been present to explain what he was looking at.

They also tore into their enemy though the damage appeared just as minimal as their own. "Olly, coordinate with the Crystal Font and ensure we both use the Protocol Seven to the fullest. I want to finish these guys quick."

"I'm working with their tech officer now," Olly replied. "We've got it installed and ready. They report all settings nominal. Our broadsides should be ready for the next round in just a second."

"All fighters are away," Adam announced. "Bombers too."

"Keep them away from our target," Gray replied. "Get them out there to cover the other alliance ships and when Clea's team is ready, they'll need an escort."

"Aye, sir." Adam conveyed the orders to Revente.

"Pulse cannons are ready, sir," Redding said.

"Excellent." Gray took a deep breath. "Initiate the Protocol Seven, Olly."

"Yes, sir." He tapped away at the computer and nodded to Redding. "Frequency established. Fire away."

"Gladly." Redding hit the button and their vessel hummed for half a second as a barrage pounded the enemy vessel. Their shields were useless, just as before and as the attack penetrated their hull, large bubbled explosions riddled the surface. The enemy cracked in half, drifted then vaporized in a massive blue-red explosion.

The shockwave shook the Behemoth but it ended quickly.

"Well done," Gray said. "How's the Crystal Font doing?"

Olly watched his scan for a moment and tilted his head. "They...they must've done it wrong." He replayed their attack and they watched as their strange pulse blasts reflected harmlessly off the enemy shields. "I'm analyzing their attack now to see what happened. I...can't believe it wouldn't have worked. That makes no sense!"

"Maybe they needed more time to adapt it to their weapons," Tim suggested.

"They've had a damn week!" Olly cried, "and I was involved the whole time! It worked, I'd bet my life on it!"

"It doesn't now," Adam said.

"Crystal Font," Gray said, "please report. What happened?"

"Protocol Seven did not work," Kale replied. "We were too slow to fire. My tech crew detected a signal sent to the other ships just as you fired your volley. We believe they were warned."

"How could they make an adjustment so quickly?" Adam shook his head. "That makes no sense! Altering their shield parameters instantly?"

"It's possible, sir," Olly said grudgingly. "It's not power efficient but it seems they're randomizing their shield frequencies in three second intervals. I have no idea how long they can keep that up but that's what they did and frankly, I bet they did it with a simple push of a button."

One of the enemy vessels moved toward the Behemoth. Gray watched for a moment, thinking. Every second counted so he didn't have time to really analyze the situation. They were in a tactical environment requiring split second decisions, the right ones to boot. He nodded once and stepped down to address the bridge crew.

"Olly, work on finding a way to adapt Protocol Seven to their little trick. If they are draining power countering us, then there must be a weakness. Find it."

Olly nodded. "Aye, sir."

"Redding, let's draw that ship away from the planet. We got them down to five ...let's see if we can even the odds."

"On it." Redding adjusted course.

"Tim, analyze the system for navigational anomalies, dead planetary bodies, debris, anything we might be able to use if we can get these guys moving. I need obstacles."

"Yes, sir."

"Adam, keep coordinating with those pilots. Get every pilot we've got ready for launch and try to keep us at seventy-five active, twenty-five resting."

"Got it."

The enemy fired at them, energy beams sizzling by their shields. "That was close!" Olly said.

"Not really," Redding replied. "I evaded. I learned a lot about them in our last engagement."

"Good show," Gray said. "Let's keep up that kind of performance and we'll get through this. Agatha, get us on coms with those other Alliance ships. We're going to need to work together. You've got your jobs, people. Let's make them happen."

Chapter 5

Olly multitasked, running an evaluation program against the enemy shield configuration and the Protocol Seven while also monitoring short range scans to track ship movement. He fed various reports to different department heads outside the bridge crew and answered messages from the Crystal Font techs who weren't as familiar with the algorithm as he was.

He felt wholly in his element.

The enemy may use brute force for the majority of their tactics but they proved to be tech savvy beyond anything Olly would've guessed. Their ability to adapt made sense. They couldn't take on a multicultural army like the alliance without being wily. This setback, and he was convinced that's all it was, made sense but wouldn't last.

Somehow, the Protocol Seven would have a method to get past this defense but his initial simulations all failed. I really need to fundamentally rewrite the code. It was designed to find their frequency and pierce through it, that's the strength. Countering the randomization would require more power and additional AI protocols to match the pattern.

Figuring out how the enemy computer ran through the task sequences might not be possible in its present state. He scanned the code, contemplating where he might modify it to make the changes. Maybe I can't have it just go right through their shields...but it may be possible to lower the integrity of their defenses.

He started a new set of simulations just as the enemy sent another attack their way. Redding didn't fully dodge this one but their shields held, keeping them safe. Olly redirected energy to reinforce those deflectors then sent a request to the engineering team to normalize power flow to that region.

Paul admitted he didn't even know he could do that in the last fight. I was probably wasted on the Tam'Dral.

"They're definitely pursuing us, Captain," Tim said. "The Crystal Font has also pulled one from the other two ships. Three to two now."

"No," Olly said. "The last one's not engaged with anyone. It's still landing troops. I'm picking up readings of drop ships deploying. They're definitely all over the ground attack."

"Adam, get the Crystal Font to join our fighters to take down some of those drop ships. Let's limit their reinforcements on the ground."

"On it."

"Harass them, Redding," Gray said. "Throw shots to keep them moving. We're giving them too easy of a time following us. Go for precision shots and Olly, how's the Protocol Seven evaluation coming?"

Olly sighed. "You won't like the answer, sir. Let me compile some more information and I'll get it to you soon. Another two minutes."

"Make it one."

"I'll do what I can." Olly frowned, working his controls swiftly. As the shots blasted by them, they returned fire. He wanted to look up but forced himself to remain focused. No time for curiosity. Let them do their jobs. I've got mine. This is fine. Everything's cool. I've got this...hopefully in one minute.

***

Agatha spoke up. "Captain, I'm receiving a transmission from the alliance ships on an emergency frequency. They're hailing us and the Crystal Font."

Gray nodded and took his seat. "Patch it into my personal station." He put an ear piece in and looked at his screen, waiting for the connection to establish. When it did, he heard a voice but received no visual.

"This is Anthar Pi'Inxi. Thank you for responding to our distress call. We are in desperate need of assistance."

Kale answered, "I'm sorry, Anthar Pi'Inxi, we did not respond to your call. We were here to visit the facility and stumbled on the fight. What happened?"

"Two ships are stationed here anyway to protect the system from incursion. They put out a distress call when they picked up enemy readings on the outskirts of the system. We arrived to find six warships pounding ours and immediately engaged. Some of us aren't doing so well...my own ship is down to sixty percent hull integrity and shields are failing."

"How many ships showed up?" Gray asked. "Was it only six?"

"Negative," Pi'Inxi replied. "They arrived with eight and we destroyed one. The other...we don't know where it went. Perhaps it's fallen into reserve. Listen to me, this is very important. We have a traitor somewhere in our midst, most likely in the facility."

"What?" Kale snapped. "How do you know this? That's a very serious allegation."

"My tech officer discovered residual data on one of the satellites. Someone tried to scrub it but failed to remove all traces of their activities. The message went directly into enemy space. Besides, you know as well as I do these research facilities are our most highly guarded secrets. There's no way they'd just stumble upon it without help."

Great, Gray thought, now we're not just dealing with an overwhelming force but a mole too. That's going to go over well. Who would side with these monsters? And why? What do they hope to gain?

"We're sending a team to the surface," Gray said. "They'll help evacuate the scientists and extract as much data as possible before destroying the facility."

"The garrison down there is taking a real pounding." Pi'Inxi sighed. "We sent down reinforcements from all our ships to bolster their numbers and they're holding for now but I can't say for how long. We wanted to support them from orbit but we've been too busy."

Gray nodded. "Understood. A small force will be able to get in and out quietly. As long as your people hold them, we've got a chance to rescue all those people. Let's coordinate our attacks on these guys and put them to bed."

"What about Protocol Seven?" Kale asked. "Why didn't it work?"

"The signal we read from the ship we destroyed told them to randomize their shield frequencies. Protocol Seven is contingent on piercing the current frequency and ignoring them. As soon as they knew to counter us, the algorithm became useless but don't worry, Olly is reverse engineering it now to try and make it effective again."

"We may have tipped our hand too soon," Kale said. "We're coordinating with your pilots as requested. Those drop ships will not make it to the surface. Good luck, my friends. We may all need it."

***

Meagan and Mick dodged aside as two enemy fighters screamed past them. Their wingmen caught the attackers in a crossfire, annihilating them with a couple bursts of pulse lasers. Zeroing in on another contingent, the wing commander let the targeting computer work its magic then pulled the trigger.

A fiery ball erupted and she nudged her controls to the left, avoiding the debris.

"Panther One, this is Giant Control. I need you and Panther Two to join up with...Tai'Li wing to take out some drop ships that are just entering orbit."

"You want us to break atmosphere?" Meagan asked. "Cause the fight's up here, sir."

"There's a big fight down there, Commander and I need you guys to slow it down. Be advised, we have received word that these vessels are armed and very tough. I'd send bombers but they aren't fast enough to catch up. It's on you."

"How many are we talking about?"

"Ten. With the four of you, it shouldn't be too hard. Do not let any of them reach the surface of their own accord."

"On it, Giant Control." Meagan switched her com wide. "Panther Wing, this is Panther One. I'm taking Panther Two on a special mission. Stay linked up with the other Behemoth wings and give these guys hell. We'll be back as soon as we can."

"Should be like shooting fish in a barrel," Mick said. "Piece of cake."

"That saying sucks," Meagan replied, dodging an attack and moving up to her wingman's left. "Poor fish."

"Yeah, I...honestly never thought much about it before..."

"Tai'Li wing, this is Panther One. What is your position?"

"Panther One, this is Tai'Li Command. My second and I are moving into the theater of operations now. Estimated Time to Engagement, twenty seconds."

Meagan brought her scans up and zeroed in on the coordinates. "If we push it, we can meet you there about the same time. Gun it, Mick."

"On it, ma'am."

Meagan hit her afterburners. Even the dampeners couldn't totally compensate and she was pressed hard into her chair. Ships flew by them, explosions and pulse blasts they narrowly missed. Twenty seconds seemed like such a short time but hip deep in conflict, it felt like an eternity. As the planet loomed ahead, she and Mick felt the beginning turbulence of atmosphere.

Noise suddenly surrounded them. Sound was possible in gravity, causing every rattle and windy rush to compete with their coms.

"Keep your wings in until we've got good air to glide on," Meagan said.

"Not my first time to dance, ma'am."

"Sorry, Mick. Old habits and all that." The shields on her nose lit up, glowing from the heat. The whole ship began bucking from entering the upper atmosphere, the wind pockets buffeting her on all sides. Up ahead, she saw the thrust tails of their targets, drop ships five times the size of her fighter. "Those are freakin' huge!"

"Scanning for weak points now," Mick said. "Tai'Li, I'm sharing...do you have this?"

"Affirmative, Panther Two." The calm voice spoke over their speakers. "We must first take out the rear and forward shields located on their bellies. Then, we can trash the engines and send them into a free fall."

"They're going to hit the ground hard," Meagan said. "I'm talking crater the size of South Carolina big."

"That's probably hyperbole," Mick said. "I hope."

"Let's just try to get them to fall on their buddies."

The two alliance ships joined them, triangles of smooth metal with extended poles for their weapons. The cockpits were invisible outwardly, making it hard to target their pilots directly. They glowed yellow from their shields and their weapons crackled with purple energy like tiny lightning bolts dancing along the extended barrels.

"Can you pierce shields with those?" Meagan asked. Their own weapons tended toward brute force. They pounded the enemy so hard it didn't matter that they were defended. Like a broadsword in the medieval times, the armor may remain intact but the bones beneath were shattered and broken.

"We will hit the shields first then switch to hull piercing shots."

"Okay, Mick and I will take the one on the left...er...marking him now on your scanners." She extended her wings and her ship leveled off, granting her better control in the new environment. Mick did the same and took up position beside her. "I've got the targets locked." A blue beam flew past her on the port side. "Whoa, they're shooting back."

"Kinda thought they would," Mick replied as he pulled an evasive maneuver, flipping his ship and gunning the engine. Meagan saw him out of the corner of her eye as he pressed forward. "Taking my first shot."

Meagan saw the weapons light up, brightening her own cockpit even over the sunlight beaming overhead, amplified by the atmosphere. Sparks flew from the drop ship and the shields flickered. A small turret, only visible on scans, picked up the pace on the shooting, firing frantically in an attempt to shake the fighters.

"That thing's on the bottom." Meagan pulled up. "Get out of its firing arc and we can finish this thing off."

"Panther One," One of the Tai'Li fighters spoke up. "We have incoming fighters. They seem to be trying to rescue their drop ships."

"Firing missiles." Meagan locked target and pulled the trigger. Her vessel lurched from the sudden discharge and two projectiles whizzed away. The drop ship lacked maneuverability and when the warheads struck the rear compartment with the shields weakened, it exploded in a fiery ball on impact. "Splash one!"

"Panthers One and Two," Tai'Li again, "continue to engage the drop ships and we will maintain your back."

"Not exactly the saying but I'll take it," Meagan replied. "Keep em busy back there. Mick, we have to pick up the pace. I'm going to do a fly by on the next shield, you blow their engines."

"Done."

Meagan jammed the throttle forward, taking the next enemy at an angle. She spun her craft sideways, making minor course corrections to avoid the turret. A quick reading on her scanner said she had good angle but instead of firing immediately, she took an extra second to draw in a second target.

Firing three good bursts, she veered away just before colliding with the drop ship, letting her burners scorch its side. Her first two hits took down the shields, the third knocked out the turret. "Wide open for you, Mick!"

Mick bombarded the vessel with his pulse blasters, annihilating it's engines and sending debris flying off into the sky. "Splash two."

"Jesus, we've got eight to go. We need to pick up this pace." Meagan's shields flared around her. "Whoa, whoa, whoa, Tai'Li, whatchya doin' back there? I thought you guys had them."

"One slipped by." An odd beam of purple energy sliced an enemy fighter in half. "We're clear to assist."

"Let's make short work of these guys." They plunged forward, approaching the next set of drop ships. We've got approximately ninety seconds before they reach the surface. We're going to cut it close.

"Crap, that turret hit me," Mick said. His calm tone made Meagan frown.

"How bad?"

"Shields absorbed it but I'm down to forty percent. That was a solid hit."

"Fall back and let them recharge. The three of us have this one."

One of the Tai'Li fighters raced ahead, saturating the drop ship with more purple energy. Electrical bolts danced off the enemy hull and the engines suddenly shut down. He fried the entire system! It plunged, powerless toward the ground. When it hit, it would be like a missile and cause just as much damage.

Meagan pulled a quick scan to see where it would land. Their luck didn't hold out. The trajectory of the falling vessel took it right into the heart of the alliance troops. Well, shit. She throttled up and fired her pulse blasters, intent to pulverize it into tiny pieces. The first five shots ripped open the hull. Enemy soldiers spilled out, their bodies rag dolling all around her.

One of the bodies bounced off her shield and caught on fire. That's just horrifying. Wow.

"Thank you, Panther One," Tai'Li command said. "I think you just saved a lot of lives."

"We're not done yet. Keep up the pressure. We have to wrap this up."

Three down, seven to go. Push it guys, push it.

***

"Panther Wing reports they are taking down the drop ships, sir," Adam said. "They should be wrapped up shortly and are going to deploy some ordinance on the troops already on the ground."

"Okay, but get them back into the air as soon as possible. Much as I want to give those guys on the ground some help, it's thick up here too." Gray paced over to Olly. "Come on, Olly. What've you got for me?"

"Redesigning code is one thing but doing so in a fire fight makes it a lot more complicated." Olly sighed. "I've got some of it going but it's going to take time to compile and test. If we screw up and try too soon, they might find a way to counter it again."

"Time's not a luxury we have but do it right." Gray turned to Redding. "How're we doing on that evasive?"

The ship shook from a direct hit.

"Not great, sir," Redding grunted. "That bastard's got us at a disadvantage. We're flying backward and he can plunge straight ahead. We need something to turn the tide of this, give him another broadside or something."

"Tim, how'd you do on cataloging the system?" Gray patted the navigator's chair.

"They keep it really clean, sir." Tim shrugged. "I never thought I'd say this, but I miss the inefficiency of our recycle and reclamation teams."

"You and me both." Gray scowled at the screen. "Okay, this is what I need you to do. We have to coordinate with the alliance better. Multiple ships blasting at these guys should make short work of them. Crystal Font, you still on the line?"

"Yes, Captain," Kale replied. "And we heard your comment. I agree. Let us gather our strength at the following coordinates, away from the planet."

"Sounds good to me." Gray turned to Redding. "Get us to those coordinates ASAP and let's put some points on the board. The longer we carry on like this, the worse it'll get." And the better chance more enemies will show up. Come on, guys. Let's get some urgency here.

Chapter 6

Clea entered the command center for ground control. Lieutenant Colonel Marshall Dupont stood amongst his aides, observing the battle raging on the planet below. She cleared her throat and approached, offering him the customary Earth salute as he acknowledged her. Now to convey Gray's orders.

"Lieutenant Colonel," she started, "Captain Atwell sent me."

"Yes, I know. He sent the order." Marshall rubbed his brow. "One of the alliance ships sent over a coded message with detailed information on where the research facility is. Even if those bastards out there knew exactly where it was, the defensive matrix would've made short work of any drop ships trying to gain easy access."

"What's that mean for us?"

"That you won't be able to go straight in."
Marshall brought up a holographic, three dimension map of the area. "I'm afraid you'll have to drop in over here both to avoid detection and fall outside the defense grid. Once on the surface, you'll make your way overland, through some pretty tough terrain, until you reach the defensive wall. The drop ship will remain in place, hidden from the enemy until you radio for it and bring it in for extract.

"The next part's on you. We don't have any idea how to overcome your technology."

Clea nodded. "I can handle that. Do we need to brief the strike team?"

"Already done." Marshall replied. "You'll be heading down with Captain Hoffner and seven other marines. Any larger contingency could be picked up on scans. We don't anticipate any conflict other than small scale skirmishes and that's all you'll be equipped for."

"What do you know about the terrain?"

"Only what your people sent. I've uploaded it to your personal scanner and those of the men. It looks like some pretty nasty foliage, potentially even dangerous and I'm not talking about poison ivy. You'll need to take care or you won't even make it to the facility."

"Understood, sir." Clea motioned for the door. "I'm going to gear up and meet the soldiers in the hangar. Can we depart soon?"

"We have clearance so mission's go ASAP." Marshall stepped closer. "You and Hoffner make sure our guys come back, one way or another, you hear me?"

"Yes, sir." Clea nodded again. "Thank you for your help."

"Gray thinks this'll work so I'm with him but if it were up to me, I'd bomb that place from orbit just to be sure."

"I'm seeing that as a common way of thinking for humans," Clea replied. "I'm glad cooler heads prevailed."

Clea left the room and ran down the hallway, dodging people as she went. When she arrived at the armory, she changed her clothes, exchanging the white pants and jacket for tactical black. Body armor went on next and she collected a rifle, fifteen extra magazines and a belt full of grenades. A helmet followed, one with a face screen that linked with her computer.

Captain Hoffner led the contingency of marines to the Tam'Dral when it first arrived. Clea respected him but didn't know him well. He seemed like a hard man but he looked out for his soldiers, putting their lives above his on many occasions, or so his record stated. When she arrived, the scowl he gave her said their relationship may not be starting off on the best foot.

"Miss An'Tufal," Hoffner said. "We received our briefing and we're ready to depart if you are."

"I am, sir." Clea nodded. The others didn't seem nearly as put out as he did. Most of them probably relished the chance to get off the ship and do something rather than wait for potential boarding actions. Whether or not that was true, she couldn't say but they walked with a spring in their step.

Hoffner grabbed her arm before she mounted the ship's ramp.

"I sure hope this isn't a fool's errand." He kept his voice low. "Those men don't need to be throwing their lives away for nothing."

"My people risked their lives for your entire race," Clea said. "I've never brought that up before but considering how little regard you and others feel about my people down there, I think it applies. Help me bring them out, Captain. That's what you and I swore to do as soldiers, isn't it?"

"Yes, protect civilians, I get it." Hoffner let her go. "Don't get me wrong, we'll perform one hundred and twenty percent but this is going to be dangerous."

"Few missions in the military are not." Clea stepped up the ramp. "I believe we have an appointment to keep."

Those already on board strapped in and stowed their gear. They carried a lot more than she anticipated but they kept their body armor as light as hers. This mission required mobility, not outright combat. She had a vague idea of what to expect when it came to the foliage. As a child, she studied carnivorous plants which managed to find their way onto several alliance worlds.

They kept them from overrunning their facilities and cities but left them in place as a natural defense against invaders. Such security worked both ways, unfortunately. Luckily, she'd been through enough survival courses to know which to avoid and if she took lead, she should be able to get them through the situation without too much trouble.

"Tower control, this is Drop Ship Zeta. We are go for launch and need fighter escort, over."

"Drop Ship Zeta, we have an escort waiting for you outside. Be sure to avoid the big pulse cannons on your starboard side. Otherwise, Godspeed and fast journey."

Clea swallowed hard, feeling a tickle of fear cling to the back of her neck. One blast from the enemy vessel would eliminate their ship. They'd die instantly, which she supposed was better than suffering but still…one shot. I hope you're keeping them busy up there, Gray. She closed her eyes as they lifted off, pulling out of the hangar and into space.

Four fighters closed around them as they picked up speed, she saw them through the windows in front and behind her. Their escort should be able to get them through the mainstay of the fighting but then again, massive starships weren't the only threat out there. Enemy fighters flew around and if they weren't engaged already, they'd be looking for targets.

One more risk that could take them down easily. Just as she was psyching herself completely out of the ability to remain calm, the ship rattled. Clea grabbed her seat and looked around, craning her neck to see where the attack came from.

"Just a rogue shot," one of the marines said. "Don't worry about it. That shit happens all the time when we go on these missions. Some jack ass misses and then we almost catch it. Usually friendly fire too."

"Friendly fire?" Clea leaned her head back. "Wouldn't that be ironic?"

"It always is," Hoffner added. "How many drop missions have you been on?"

"Alliance drop ships are quite different than these," Clea said. "But in my own military, I've been through more than thirty."

"Newbie," one of the marines scoffed. "This'll make one hundred and seventeen for me."

"How many of you guys have been through a drop ship crash?" Another asked. All hands went up but Clea's. "Ah, shit. She's due."

"Damn it, lady!" A random voice complained.

"No, I'm not due," Clea shook her head emphatically. "Seriously, I don't think I need to experience a crash."

"You'd better hope fate agrees."

Hoffner waved them quiet. "Stop the superstitious BS. We're almost into the combat zone."

Clea looked outside again and saw the chaos of space battle raging just ahead. Their ship pushed on, plunging right through a massive skirmish between too many fighters to count. Blasts whizzed by, cooking their shields and even splashing off their hull a few times. Luckily, the drop ships were particularly tough and ready to take some serious punishment.

One of their escort had to break off to engage an enemy looking for an easy kill. Clea held her breath as she watched them dance about before the Earth fighter got the better angle and lit up his opponent. The blue-purple globe barely died down before they had their escort back, taking his position again to the right.

These people are incredible at their jobs, Clea thought. I'm lucky to have them so close by…good thing they took my request seriously.

Speed increased and the gravitational force pushed everyone into their seats. All action outside the window became a blur, even the distant stars streaked by. Clea felt her stomach rebel, dancing about in retaliation against the physical trauma the flight put on her. Though she'd been in thirty drops before, it had been years since the last one.

I don't think it would be a good idea to tell these people that now.

"We'll be out of this rough stuff in less than a minute." The pilot spoke as another blast rocked their ship. "Then the real ride begins."

The Behemoth drop ships were large enough to carry thirty soldiers into battle. With only eight, it felt terribly empty. This meant they had plenty of room for those they needed to evacuate, providing everything went according to plan. As they rapidly approached the world, something dawned on Clea, a thought she wished she could easily shove away.

This may well be a one way trip, a suicide mission resulting in all their deaths. If they failed, so much more would be lost than just their lives too. The people, their research and many military advantages of the alliance would be gone. However the enemy planned to use the data, it wouldn't bode well for anyone.

There's no failing here. We have to make this work. One way or another...

"Entering atmosphere now. Escort, we have picked up three fighters. Please engage."

Clea clenched her fists as the ship began bucking, shaking as if it had been thrown into an Earth washing machine. She lost her perspective of up or down. Vertigo closed on her senses. She shut her eyes and tried desperately to find a Zen place, any sort of quiet thought to quell her fear.

Unfortunately, the distraction around her was too great. Sound returned as they broke through to gravity and she heard blasts going off around them then explosions. Our escort? The enemy? Damn it, I can't even look at my scanner to tell!

A battle raged around them and those sitting aboard were helpless throughout. A turret on board began firing, warming the air around her. She hadn't realized how cold it became until the heat poured on. She went from goosebumps to sweat in seconds, a state which left her more miserable.

I can't believe it's possible to feel worse!

"Thank you, escort," The pilot announced. "We have shaken our tails and are approaching the landing zone. Prep yourselves for a hard landing. To avoid ground scans, we're going in fast and hot. Engines won't engage until the last second."

Oh heaven above, Clea closed her eyes again. I know this is necessary but I feel like a real idiot coming on this mission. Clearly, I needed to train more. How would I have known I needed to prepare myself for these kinds of missions? Bridge staff don't tend to leave the ship. I guess I get to be the exception to the rule.

"Five seconds to thruster burn." The pilot sounded so calm, Clea wanted to smack him. How could he maintain such a reserve considering the turbulence and thought of crashing into the ground at mach...whatever? She planned to ask him someday. "Two...One...Initiating burn."

Clea cried out as the ship lurched against the massive thrust the pilot employed. The G forces were incredible, making every muscle in her body ache and her teeth seem to come alive. Another few moments passed as the pressure became even greater then, they hit the ground with an ear shattering crash then...stillness.

Clea held her breath, wondering if she was still alive.

"Thank you for flying Zeta Airlines," the pilot announced. "We have landed safely and are ready for you to disembark. Please camouflage this vessel on your way out and good luck on your mission. We'll be waiting for your call."

One of the marines removed Clea's straps and pulled her to her feet. "C'mon. It's time to get moving."

Clea nodded, slinging her weapon and heading unsteadily for the door. Hoffner stopped her, allowing her to walk slower with him. "Easy there. I didn't want to say anything in front of them, but I'm guessing you haven't done a combat drop in a long time."

"No," she replied. "I sure haven't."

"I can tell. Regain your bearings here. We've got a few minutes while they get the ship covered. Do you know where we're going?"

"It's on our scanners. When we get outside, I'll plot us a course to keep us safe from the plant life. I haven't been specifically here before, but I have dealt with this type of terrain. Providing we're careful, it shouldn't be a problem."

"I'll hold you to it." Hoffner moved to the ramp and checked his scanner. "Surface temperature's no treat. Thirty-two celsius. Going to be a sticky romp to the base."

"The environment in jungle settings helps mask technology," Clea explained. "Casual scans pick up so much life interference they can't distinguish the fake from the real. It's just one more security measure."

"Pity there's a traitor out there who screwed all those things up."

Clea's heart burned at the thought but she nodded. "I can't imagine what they're thinking but I hope to find out why they did it."

"I've been around long enough to know betrayal rarely has a good reason," Hoffner replied. "And even when there is one, finding out doesn't satisfy the victims. Best to just deal with it and move on. It's the one time motivation doesn't make any difference."

"I'll keep that in mind, Captain." Clea stretched. She felt a semblance of normalcy falling over her. "I'm ready. Let's get out there and figure out what direction we're going. As you said, it's going to be a hike so we'll need to move as quickly as possible."

Hoffner nodded and gestured for her to go. So the mission begins, Clea thought. Let's hope my survival skills aren't as pathetic as my drop ship experience.

Chapter 7

The Crystal Font kept their distance from the ship they were battling, hammering it with ordinance Gray had never seen. He checked the readings and couldn't believe the power output but it didn't detract the vessel who took the blows. The enemy didn't care about taking damage, only winning. It gave them a slight and dangerous advantage.

Their own opponent backed off, returning to formation to blast at the four alliance ships protecting the planet. They must have an operational parameter not allowing them to get too far from their objective. The Behemoth weighed more than any other vessel in the system and they probably possessed more armor but if they had to endure what those alliance ships did, they wouldn't survive.

They needed to relieve the pressure as soon as possible.

Their allies protecting the planet gave as good as they got, holding the line like true professionals. Gray directed Redding to take the flank of the enemy, moving for a firing solution on their engines. The shields should've been weakest back there and they had to pick who they wanted to show their asses to: the lone ship or the four holding the line.

"Captain, the Crystal Font just tore down the shields of their opponent," Olly announced. "It's...hold on. I'm picking up a massive energy surge." Gray stepped over to look over his shoulder but didn't know what he was looking at.

"What is it?"

"Oh my God!" Olly tapped at the controls. "Agatha, I just took operational control of the coms." He shouted into his headset, "to all alliance vessels and Behemoth fighters, scatter! Get away from the advancing warship. It's set it's reactor to overload! It's going to blow!"

"Are you sure?" Gray stared at the screen, eyes narrow. "Why? What's..."

"I read Paul's report," Olly said. "That's why I knew what the increase in power output was. They're going to sacrifice themselves to open a lane to the planet. If all those ships don't get out of the way, they'll be crippled at best or torn apart..."

"Did they respond to your hail?"

"Agatha, back to you," Olly said. "I'm transferring back to Agatha."

Agatha tapped her controls. "Sir, they've acknowledged and are attempting to move."

"They're not going to make it!" Olly shouted. "I'm trying to access the enemy drive...see if I can shut it down."

"Can you do that?" Adam asked.

Olly swallowed hard and shook his head. "I doubt it but it's the only thing I can think to try."

"Do whatever you can." Gray watched the scanners. "They're not moving fast enough. Agatha, emphasize the importance of getting the hell out of there."

"On it, sir." Agatha started speaking firmly into the microphone.

"Olly..." Adam said. "Come on!"

"This is pretty much impossible, sir! I mean, I'm trying to hack an alien technology totally on the fly! I'm sorry!"

"Go back to working on Protocol Seven," Gray said. "They'll move in time."

"Our fighters report they are out of the blast radius," Agatha said. "Crystal Font reports the same."

"What about the other vessels? Have they even given the order?"

"Yes, sir." Agatha "The smaller ships have retreated."

"That's good for something." Gray turned to Redding. "Are we in range?"

"Five seconds."

"Fire at will as soon as we're in range." Gray sat back down. "See what we can do to distract them at least. I don't want to get close to that damn bomb."

They watched on the view screen, seemingly in slow motion as the enemy vessel plowed in the midst of the four alliance ships. Redding depressed the trigger, firing on the nearest enemy with a full barrage of pulse cannons. Shields flashed, the engines flared and popped causing the target to list.

At the same time, the enemy vessel exploded in a spectacular fashion, sending a shockwave out in every direction. Gray turned away as the flash of light filled their screen, nearly blinding him. Internal communications went crazy, turning to static for a good five seconds. When their visual came back, the carnage was unbelievable.

The alliance ships may not have been destroyed but they didn't look good. "Olly, report!"

"Three of our ships are totally crippled." Olly shook his head. "The fourth..."

"What?" Adam prompted. "What is it?"

"Life support is down, engines are offline, power is fading fast..." Olly clenched his fist. "It was closest to the enemy ship when the reactor blew."

"But the other ships?" Gray asked. "Life signs?"

"They've taken casualties and I can bring up individual damage reports soon but they are still marginally functional. Not combat effective." Olly checked something. "No, but with some repairs, they'll be mobile again."

"Okay," Gray motioned to Agatha. "Get the Crystal Font back online."

"They're on speaker, sir."

"Thanks." Gray cleared his throat. "Crystal Font, we need to organize a search and rescue for those ships but it looks like we're it now. Opinion?"

"It looks like you managed to severely damage one of them and they took care of their own. We're down to three of them with a fourth out there somewhere." Anthar Ru'Xin paused. "I believe we can handle this situation still. The majority of my people's fighters survived the explosion. We can resupply them here."

"Okay." Gray nodded, turning to Olly. "Did we truly disable that ship?"

"No," Redding answered for him. "I got at least one if not two of their engines but they're moving now. They've been pelting us with turrets but so far, minimal damage."

"I concur," Olly said. "But if they turn, they're going to hit us with their cannons…and they're definitely turning."

"Redding, try to keep us behind them as best you can." Gray pointed to Adam. "Contact Revente. Get his bombers over here so we can finish this guy off."

"On it." Adam returned to his station.

The other ships began shifting their attention, two turned to face the Crystal Font and the Behemoth. Their damaged ship stopped attempting to turn and used what engine power it could muster to press toward the planet. "Keep on that bastard!" Adam shouted. "Don't let him get away!"

"Belay that," Gray said. "Much as I want to wipe them out, we have bigger fish to fry. I want you to collaborate with the Crystal Font so we can keep them busy while we perform the search and rescue operations. If there are any people left out there, they won't have much time. Let's put it to good use."

***

Meagan spun at the last second, narrowly avoiding debris from the final drop ship. As it disintegrated off to the left, she redirected her course for the enemy soldiers causing so much trouble on the ground. Mick pulled up beside her and the two Tai'Li fighters took up the rear. They dropped down low, skimming the tops of the tallest trees.

"Estimated time to theater of operation," Meagan checked her scan. "Thirty seconds."

"Panther One, this is Giant Control."

"Go ahead," Meagan said, "but make it quick. We're about to unload on some runners."

"You only have time for one volley," Giant Control replied. "Afterward, break atmosphere and get your ass back up here."

"What happened?"

"The enemy pulled a kamikaze and took out three of the alliance ships. We're trying to keep the rest of the bastards busy while we perform some search and rescue. I need you guys to rejoin your wing and get on patrol."

"Understood." Meagan shook her head. "Sorry, ground pounders. We'll do what we can. You heard them, Mick...Tai'Li...um...guys? One pass and we're back topside."

"Seems a shame," Mick said. "We could really do some damage."

"They might have some real ground to air ordinance," Meagan replied. "So we probably should be thankful we won't be giving them juicy targets to pop."

"The battleground's coming up on visual," Mick said. "Jesus Christ, do you see them all?"

Meagan squinted then leaned back in her seat. There were hundreds, possibly more, soldiers on the ground charging a fixed emplacement set up by the alliance. Their IFF lit up, showing blue on the left where a much smaller contingency tried to fend them off and red where the massive force congregated.

"Good lord, you're not kidding." Meagan sighed. "Let's do what we can."

She jerked her control back to avoid topping a tree then plunged down, firing her pulse cannons into the densest part of the crowd. Mick did the same and the Tai'Li fighters spread out to either side for maximum spread. They weren't quite close enough to see the whites of their eyes, but she sure saw them react.

The first blasts threw bodies high into the air. It caused panic and the soldiers began running, trying to spread out to avoid the heaviest casualties but there was nowhere for them to go. While they might've overrun the position they were taking with sheer numbers, those numbers provided a target rich environment.

Craters appeared where bodies once were. Corpses became obstacles they had to clamber over to escape their own deaths. Two passes would've been devastating. Meagan thought as she came to the end of the line. Half of her considered trying another fly by on their way out when her scanner picked up an incoming missile.

"Do you see that?" Meagan called out. "Mick?"

"Yeah, some prick down there had the weapons you were worried about. I've got one on me too."

"Us as well," Tai'Li added. "We have countermeasures."

"Yeah, us too." Meagan sighed. "Alright, let's follow orders and get topside. Allow their stupid missiles to get close then drop your ECM. Sync up on that too."

Their countermeasures would distract the missiles and give them a chance to pull far enough away from the missiles to avoid being blown to hell. However, if they didn't all drop them, there was a good chance the attacking rocket would change course and go after the bigger target. What was worse would be if they didn't sync up, the missile could bounce between targets, not allowing any fighter to escape.

Her scans beeped, giving her a countdown. As the clouds above broke way to blue sky, she gunned her throttle. "Countdown," Meagan shouted. "Three...two...one, fire!"

They dropped their ECM and pulled away from one another, separating out to allow their defensive measures to do their jobs. As the sky turned from blue to gray and eventually to black, the scans suggested her missile drifted back and went after her defense. "I'm clear!" She called out. "Mick, report!"

"Mine's good."

"I haven't dropped mine," Tai'Li One said. "It's tight on my tail."

"I'll try to cut it off," Tai'Li Two replied. "Stay on course."

"Don't try it," Meagan said. "You won't be able to target that thing at this speed while climbing with gravity. Chances are good it'll turn on you."

"You aren't in command of us." Tai'Li Two spoke again. "If I don't help him, he dies. He'd do the same for me. Continue on course, Human. We'll meet you if we can."

"Tai'Li?" Meagan couldn't see what was happening specifically but her scanners showed blips approaching the friendly vessel. They'd turned their coms to a different frequency. "God damn it, Mick, can you see them?"

"No, but that missile's really freakin' close..."

Meagan felt her ship shake just as she broke atmosphere. Her wings retracted and she tapped her scanner screen for a rear view. A massive explosion sat a thousand feet or so behind her. Was that one of them or the missile?

"Panther One, this is Tai'Li One." Meagan let out a sigh of relief. "We have destroyed the missile and are heading for the rendezvous."

"Way to cut it close there, Tai'Li," Mick answered for her. "Good work and we'll see you on the other side."

"Not the best choice of words, Mick." Meagan shook her head. "But point taken." She looked out over the carnage around them, the damaged alliance ships drifting nearby and the brilliant lights of conflict raging off in the distance. It gave her a heavy feeling in her stomach, a sense of grandeur she didn't get in their last engagement.

As they passed by the conflict zone, she throttled up. "Let's hurry up," she said. "I want to be closer to allies ASAP."

"Yeah..." Mick sounded somber. "I know exactly how you feel."

Chapter 8

Clea watched as the men finished camouflaging the ship. From the air, it would be impossible to see it and the cloth provided protection against active scans. Someone would have to literally stumble upon it. Providing they hurried, there'd be no risk of that. The enemy soldiers were occupied with fortified emplacements, at least for a while.

Hoffner turned to her. "Okay, now that we're ready, what's the plan?"

Clea checked her computer. Once she disembarked the vessel, she initiated a program to plot a course through the jungle to the facility. It worked off of satellite scans, taking in the most recent data and calculating all available paths to their destination. The lines were color coded with green being the easiest and red being nearly impossible.

"It depends," Clea said. "If we do not want to do any trail blazing, we'll have to stick to a couple of specific routes. Unfortunately, those are established through activity by the inhabitants of the planet and thus closer to what I'd call the current battlefield. It could put us at risk of enemy encounters, though perhaps not large enough to matter."

"Okay, what about the not so easy ones?"

"Those require us to cut through some of the jungle ourselves, which presents a hardship as well. You see, some of the foliage is dangerous and can be as bad as having to fight. Personally, I prefer and recommend we go for something in the middle. Limit the amount of cutting we have to do."

"What about predators?" Hoffner asked. "Do we have to worry about alien animals giving us a hard time?"

"Survey of the planet suggests most animals are afraid of people and won't be a bother," Clea explained. "There are enough of us living on the planet who venture out into the wilderness for research or recreation to keep them at bay but that's not to say we won't encounter something. I'll have my active scanner going the whole time."

"Okay." Hoffner turned to the men. "Listen up, people. We're moving out. This place isn't safe. We've got enemy soldiers, killer plants and God knows what else. Our objective, as you know, is rescue and recovery. Let's stick together, be wary and stay alive. If any of you die out here, consider yourself on report. You got it?"

"Yes, sir." They didn't shout but still managed to include some enthusiasm in their voices. Hoffner nodded once. "Alright, Jenks and Walsh, you take point. The rest of you stagger back two by two. An'Tufal, you're with me."

Clea took up a position beside the captain, her head on a swivel. One of the most important tenants she remembered from her survival training involved situational awareness. You can't rely solely on scans, the instructor said. Eyes and ears are just as important. You may not have your other senses in armor or environmental suits but use what you've got. It could save your life.

The shuttle set down in a small clearing amidst thick trees covered in vines and moss. The ground itself was soft from meters of crushed leaves and mold. As she gestured in the direction they needed to go, she looked at the sky then turned to the path she'd decided upon. Once they stepped into the jungle, the canopy would blot out the sun.

Each of them wore only light armor but even that provided enough environmental protection to offset the heat. Her computer showed that it was thirty-five degrees celsius with eighty-seven percent humidity. Losing their suits would make this an incredibly miserable trip and she already felt moisture clinging to her clothes and helmet.

Fortunately, their face screens were specially designed to not fog up or they'd be unable to see anything at all. As they stepped out of the sun, the dim glow of light shining through patches above made the scene eerie but it was far from silent. They heard cries of birds and other animals, all out of sight but surrounding them on every side.

"This place is cheery," one of the marines said. She had no idea which one. "Kind of like a vid with the ape man guy."

"Can it," Hoffner said. "Focus or one of those things out there will eat your ass for lunch."

Clea didn't disagree. Any predators willing to get close to them would definitely enjoy one of them for a meal. She'd heard of such things but in a mostly civilized area such as the research facility, she couldn't imagine they'd encounter much. Her bigger fear came from the carnivorous plants. Those were hard to identify and tended to kill quick.

"How long will it take to get to our destination?" Hoffner asked.

"At present speed, just over an hour," Clea replied. "I'm estimating not much more or less as we'll undoubtedly face delays and windfalls."

"Jesus, I hoped to get a lot closer."

"We'd tip off the enemy if we closed in too much. They're in the general area after all."

Hoffner nodded but didn't seem happy. She understood. The humans proved to want tangible information before every mission. Their desire for solid intelligence made little sense to her though. They were often forced to improvise because what they thought they knew turned out to be false.

Her own people did the research then relied on skill and resourcefulness to tackle missions. It put her at odds with Gray a few times in their earlier career, mostly on a hypothetical level. She deferred to him in all things aboard the Behemoth but when they debated, she pushed her opinion much harder.

A few bouts like that and she felt she grew as an officer, both tactically and strategically.

"What is that?" one of the men said. "Did you see something move up ahead?"

Everyone aimed their weapons in the general area up ahead of them. Leaves rustled. "Hold your fire," Hoffner said. "No one pulls a trigger unless I say."

Clea tapped at her scanner, using the HUD in her helmet to read the results. A close check of the area revealed a life form nearby, something small. The device provided a picture from the animal database and she let out a sigh of relief. "Stand down." She sent the image to the other soldiers, that of a colorful bird. "It's not dangerous."

"Move out, people." Hoffner sounded annoyed but nodded at Clea.

Two hundred yards into the bush, the terrain became more difficult to traverse. Jenks and Walsh cut a path through, their rifles slung on their backs. Clea double checked their path and they were on course for what should've been only moderately difficult. Imagine what the hard one would've looked like.

Her scans indicated the growth occurred in less than two days. Forty-eight hours generated the obstacles, which seemed fast enough to watch it if one was patient. She looked up and wondered how much taller the vines were than the day before. One consolation for such robust foliage involved it hampering the enemy just as much as them.

But it's going to slow us down a lot more than I thought. I'll recalculate our ETA and factor in additional trail blazing.

Half an hour later, they cleared a path and made decent time. Jenks and Walsh stopped suddenly on a small rise, staring out to their right. The rest of the men lined up with them as Hoffner and Clea joined them. A break in the trees offered a stupendous view of a valley some five miles away.

A skirmish had broken out between alliance personnel and the enemy. Every marine knew what those things were capable of now after the intruders on the ship. They'd all been briefed and shown the videos. Even the most arrogant and abrasive amongst them considered the danger they represented with respect.

They witnessed a small skirmish, a battle away from the mainstay conflict raging in some valley nearby. As the enemy cut a swath of destruction through the alliance troops, the brutality fell nothing short of shocking. Limbs flew in the air, bodies were hewn in half and several men were decapitated.

"We might be able to get there before they lose," one of the marines said. "Provide some backup."

"We cannot," Clea said. "Even if we were able, our mission is to extract the civilians and keep the data out of enemy hands."

"They're your people!" The guy shouted, advancing on her. "And you're just watching them get slaughtered!"

Clea hesitated for half a moment. "Only because we're not moving. We have to go."

"What kind of—" The man's comment got cut off by Hoffner.

"You heard the woman," Hoffner said. "We have a job to do and we're not going to finish it by standing around jaw jacking. Get your asses in gear. Now!"

Clea took up pace beside him as they started off again, moving at a brisk pace.

"I don't know about these alliance guys," a random voice said. "She didn't even care about her people, man."

"Come on, do you think us eight could've done much about that?" Random voice two spoke up. "Care has nothing to do with it. Be practical for a minute."

"Those soldiers were doing their jobs so we can do ours," Random voice three added.

"Getting slaughtered without backup?" Random voice one retorted. "Sounds noble."

"You realize we would've died down there, right?" Random voice three snapped. "That we're wearing light armor for this pleasant little hike?"

"If I would've been down there, I would've wanted some help, that's all." Random voice one again.

"You just want to blame someone." Random voice four jumped in. "And that doesn't help shit. Drop it, man. You're not winning many allies here."

"Speak for yourself," Random voice five decided he had opinions too. "I, for one don't give much of a crap about this planet. I think we should've stayed home."

"God, not that again." Random voice two lamented. "You've been complaining since we got our orders."

"As should you," Five said. "This is a BS assignment and we shouldn't be out here."

"You need a new line, man," Three added. "I'm sick of the same stuff out of your mouth day after day."

"I'm sick of all this talking," Hoffner said. "Now shut your traps and focus! Jesus, I'd be shocked if the entire planet doesn't know we're here! Next man who speaks without reporting something is getting a demerit."

Clea thought about their concerns, wondering about perspective. Men like these, marines on the ground, never seemed to have the high level view. Even those who agreed with the vision of their leaders did so out of faith and trust rather than understanding. The ramifications of the research facility data falling into enemy hands reached much farther than an alliance inconvenience.

If the enemy employed the information, they'd have a Protocol Seven style advantage only theirs wouldn't fail. They'd know everything about how alliance weapons are designed and planned, how the ships are constructed and the structural weaknesses. So many little things which would amount to a catastrophe.

I wish I could explain that to these men so they understood why they are here.

They didn't want to hear it though. Each of them harbored their own feelings and prejudices, their passions, strengths and weaknesses. Those who took up arms the way they did tended to be far less interested in grand campaigns. They cared about surviving, getting the job done and getting home.

Justifying the job might matter if they lost someone but in the midst of it, they just wanted to get in and get out. Clea agreed with that part of the mentality however, she always viewed the big picture. If someone had assigned her this task, she would've known, through common sense, the value of what they wanted her to save.

Of course, if people honestly thought bombing the facility from orbit was a good idea, then there'd be no convincing them. Hypocritical thinking at its finest. The same people who didn't mind annihilating the base and all its inhabitants were the same ones who wanted to rush in to help soldiers in a hopeless battle.

She'd encountered plenty of that from humans in the past. They could dispassionately suggest the destruction of a thing and in the same breath act selflessly. Such dichotomy made little sense to Clea and much as she tried to understand, she eventually gave up. Many ideals humans lived by confused her. Their duality most of all.

The road went both ways. She knew she confounded some of the humans as well. Since the day she joined them as their liaison officer, she knew she'd have an uphill battle winning friends or expressing herself in a way they understood. Some of them tried, some didn't but it took her months before any of them really warmed up to her.

Clea never blamed any of them. They'd just had a hostile encounter with aliens and another alien joined them shortly after. None of them had a chance to mourn their losses before they were faced with more unknown, another strange factor to consider as they moved forward into a vast and dangerous universe—one they didn't even know existed.

Humans can only tolerate so much change before they react violently. Luckily for her, they had a focus for their rage. History showed what they did when they grew tired of paradigm shifts. When the alliance ships left and she became a lone Kielan among so many humans, she harbored plenty of fear. It proved to be unfounded for the most part but there were still some who did not like her solely because she was different.

"Jenks!" Walsh's voice tore Clea from her reverie and she looked sharply ahead. The other marines spread out, aiming their weapons. She joined Hoffner as he rushed forward. Her scanner read clear.

They reached the edge of a gaping hole. Jenks was at the bottom, light from the top right of his armor beaming up at them. "What the hell happened?" Hoffner demanded.

"I was in lead," Jenks replied. "And the ground just gave way right beneath me."

"Are you hurt?"

"I should be...but I'm not." He directed their attention to pointed sticks roughly half a meter long sticking up all around him. "Miracle I didn't get impaled."

"They don't look too fresh," Walsh said. "These are kind of old, sir."

"You might've been saved by the fact this is a really old trap." Hoffner looked around. "Get him out of there and let's keep moving but this will definitely slow us down. If we have to worry about that kind of thing on top of the predators, carnivorous plants and potential enemy contact..."

Clea nodded. "I know, sir."

Hoffner pulled her aside and switched their coms to private. Still, he whispered, "what could've dug that? Do you know of any other indigenous life here?"

"No, sir." Clea shook her head. "I scanned the entire planet with their satellites. If there's anything here, it knows how to go unnoticed from advanced technology. However, I believe they must have died out or been gone for a while. You saw the state of that."

"I'm kind of surprised it wasn't filled in." Hoffner hummed.

"Sir, it was." Clea patched her scan over to his helmet. "As you can see, those sticks extended four meters into the ground but we only saw half a meter. Plus, he only fell two meters. I believe that ditch was quite a bit larger and far more frightening when it was made."

"Jesus..." Hoffner sighed. "At least it wasn't as dangerous as it could've been. I wonder how clever these natives were. Let's hope they stuck to shovels and sticks." He turned to the marines who had just helped Jenks out of the hole. "Alright, people we have another threat to worry about and the next one might not be mostly ruined. Stay frosty."

"Hard to do in this climate, Captain," Walsh replied. The long stare he received made him lift a hand. "Not the best time for a joke, sir. Sorry about that."

"Just get going."

Clea fell in behind them, adjusting her scans for the new variable. She had no idea if she'd be able to detect dangers before they happened but it would be nice. How long ago had the creatures who did this disappeared? Perhaps they had more information at the facility. Her sister harbored a keen interest in xenobiology.

The thought of her sibling made her deflate and her stomach do a flip. She wanted the older woman to be okay, to ensure she was safe but her irrational nerves at seeing her again wouldn't die down. Both of them had a job to do and Clea knew that took priority over any emotional attachment or reunion.

I just hope you're okay, sister. I'm coming. Just hang on a little longer.

Chapter 9

"Another direct hit on our starboard bow," Redding said. "Olly?"

"Shields holding," Olly replied. "I'm manually regulating the shields. It's a trick I picked up from Protocol Seven. By fluctuating the frequency, I can enhance the integrity of our defenses...well, considerably."

"Keep giving it to them," Gray said. "Don't let up."

"Search and Rescue ships have arrived at the alliance vessels," Agatha said. "They're reporting little enemy activity in the area."

"Cause we're keeping them all busy," Adam muttered.

"Enemy shields down!" Olly shouted. "Hit them hard, Redding! Go!"

Redding unleashed the pulse cannons, turning the ship sharply to give them a second barrage from the other side. The enemy ship began to list, drifting away from them before cracking at several points. Bodies were torn through the hull breaches and as the ship divided completely in half, something exploded cascading an orange ball before going dark.

"One down, two to go," Gray said. "Not doing too bad, huh?"

"At least we've evened the odds," Adam said. "Again."

"The Crystal Font has started harassing the ship that was landing troops. Reinforcements to the surface have been totally stopped." Olly tapped away at the console. "They've engaged and the final ship is moving toward us."

"Good, we can wrap this up." Gray sat down.

"Captain," Agatha called, "I'm picking up a signal riding a frequency I didn't even know existed."

"What?" Gray turned. "What do you mean?"

"I was monitoring communications and saw an anomaly so I cleaned it up and tapped in. It's an enemy com link." She worked the controls for several moments. "I've recorded it and putting it through the translator. If it's our opponents, the alliance database has quite a bit of their language documented. I might be able to get the rudimentary message."

"It's probably a mayday," Adam said. "From one of the enemy ships."

Agatha shook her head. "No, sir. It's coming from outside the system."

"That's why you've never seen the frequency," Olly said. "Because they're using FTL communications. You know what this means?"

Tim spoke up, "that they have a buoy of some kind out here...probably dropped by one of their own ships."

"Right!" Olly nodded. "They brought a booster to speak to someone outside the system."

"Essentially giving their entire fleet the coordinates for this place." Gray ran his hands through his hair. "Okay then, that makes this more exciting than it needs to be. White, have you translated?"

"Only the beginning, sir. They're talking about...being here...yes, they'll be here soon." Agatha really scrutinized her screen. "They mention a time frame...I'm translating the alliance part now too...oh my...six hours."

"What's in six hours?" Adam stood. "They'll be here in six hours?"

"Their fleet." Agatha nodded. "Apparently, a vessel left the sector with the coordinates and the info they needed to lock on to the buoy."

Gray leaned back in his seat. "We have that much time to pick up the researchers and their data then get the hell out of here. Not to mention the rescue op." He nodded to Agatha. "Tell that to the Crystal Font right now. We'll need to pick up the pace and finish these two jokers off fast. It seems our hand has officially been forced. Let's make it not matter, people."

***

Kale paced the bridge of the Crystal Font, watching the battle unfold through the view screen. They seemed to be making good headway and though it would be absurd to call it a decisive victory, between his ship and the Behemoth, they certainly proved to be quite successful. Two enemies remained and with such even odds, he felt confident.

"Anthar," Wena, his communication's Zanthari spoke up. "The Behemoth just sent us a message from a known enemy frequency. Hostile reinforcements are coming and will be here in four point five casons. It seems to be an entire fleet."

"I see." Kale frowned. This left them precious little time to finish their multiple missions. I hope Clea and her marines are up to the task down there. We won't be any help. "We need to buy time for rescue ops and the soldiers on the ground. Order all pilots to resupply now and get back to our damaged vessels."

Kale returned to his seat and read the reports of current activities. Search and rescue only just began operations and ground forces stated they were in danger of being overrun. If not for the timely strafing by four fighters, and the destroyed drop ships, they'd already be dead. He pinched the bridge of his nose and tried to settle his nerves.

This wasn't supposed to be a combat zone. The thought came unbidden. After the battle where his mentor died, alliance high command summoned him immediately. He figured they were going to demote him or at the very least offer a reprimand. Some part of him thought he might even be to blame for the loss of all those alliance personnel.

When they promoted him and gave him command of the Crystal Font, he thought he must be dreaming. The blood of his friend was barely cold and he took his place. He made it sound cold in his head but he knew the old Anthar would've approved. Kale worked toward this goal his entire life…he just wished he'd achieved it differently.

Many captains would've been offended by the assignment to visit Earth but Kale welcomed a little peace. Stretching into the role of Anthar without having to fire a weapon appealed to him. As they entered Sol, he longed for the days his father talked about, those of exploration and discovery. That was his calling...he just happened to be good at conflict.

Arriving in the combat zone above the research facility shocked him but he didn't let it slow his resolve. He continued to struggle with a hint of anxiety, worry that he might not be up to the task. Employing every ounce of discipline he possessed allowed him to press on. Those around him probably had no idea he felt genuine fear at being in another major battle.

Even if it seemed like they were doing well.

He'd seen the enemy perform a sacrifice before and made his report on it. The fact his own military didn't react quickly to it surprised him. The next time he sent information to command, he'd emphasize it dramatically in bold with underlines and excessive punctuation if necessary. Even if they saved sixty percent of the people, many died who did not have to.

"Captain," Vinthari Du'Zha spoke up, his pilot and gunner. "The enemy is attempting to fall back toward the natural satellite of the planet. Shall I give chase?"

Kale squinted at the screen, rubbing his chin. Where do you think you're going? They rarely fled but occasionally, the enemy liked to regroup or draw impatient opponents into a trap. "What's the other one doing?"

"They appear to be on the same trajectory."

Kale nodded. "Is the Behemoth giving pursuit?"

"Negative, sir."

"Wena, put the humans on speaker again." Kale stood.

"They are live, sir."

"Behemoth," Kale began, "it appears our enemies are off to regroup. Do you have anything on your scanners at this time?"

"One moment," Captain Atwell replied. "We're checking."

Kale turned to his own tech officer, Deva Thi'Noch. "Do you detect anything?"

"They are moving toward a large energy reading," Deva replied. "Certainly large enough to be another ship."

"So their reserve did not leave the system after all...they must not have had to in order to send their message for help." Kale nodded. "That puts us back to three to one."

"With one injured," Deva replied. "I do not recommend getting too close to the Behemoth. The enemy may take us as a target of opportunity for another sacrifice."

"We won't be letting them do that again today." Kale spoke again to the Behemoth. "Did you get the readings?"

"Affirmative," Captain Atwell replied. "Looks like we're back up to an unfair fight."

"More than you know. The new vessel has not been damaged at all and should be at full resources." Kale tapped his leg. "This works to our advantage for now. Our pilots can operate without worry about capital ship involvement. They will need to destroy the enemy fighters before trying to transport people back to our vessels."

"Agreed." Captain Atwell paused a moment. "Our bombers didn't have a chance to do much against the ship we threw down with earlier. They're currently redeployed to assist with the debris. Have your pilots coordinate with them to gain access to parts they wouldn't otherwise be able to reach."

"Thank you, Captain." Kale motioned to Wena. "Broadcast that message."

"I trust we're going to be heading into another fight with these guys," Captain Atwell said. "This time away from the planet."

"Yes," Kale agreed. "Keep your distance from us so they don't blow up...wait a moment..." Kale grinned. "I think I may have an idea but it's not risk free. Captain, I'm going to put you onto a private channel with me to discuss it. Should only take a moment but I recommend you step off your bridge."

"Alright..." Captain Atwell agreed. "Give me just a moment."

Kale turned to Du'Zha. "You have the con. I'll be right back." He headed into the antechamber of his ready room, closing the door to initiate the com. This may well be your most insane idea yet...but they won't expect it. Here's to hoping we can pull it off.

***

Gray turned to Adam. "Hold the bridge, do not engage until I get back. I'll be in the hall for just a moment."

"Captain..."

Gray held up his finger and gave the other man a stern look. "I'll be back."

In the hallway, he patched through to Kale's private com. "What's going on?"

"Captain, I apologize for the secrecy. As you know, there's a traitor somewhere in our midst. I don't believe they are with your crew but mine...well, where there's one, there may be more."

"Understood." Gray frowned. "So what did you want to discuss?"

"A gamble, one which may win us a keen advantage but it's going to be quite dangerous." Kale paused a moment. "As you know, the enemy has proven themselves quite willing to sacrifice their people and their ships. They do so when the opportunity presents itself to cause massive amounts of damage."

"Yes, they definitely take a lack of self preservation to new and horrible places."

"Precisely. The Behemoth and Crystal Font are all that stand in the way of them taking over this system. They have three vessels...one would be more than enough to mop up here and get them home. Therefore, if they see a chance to take us out..."

"They'll happily throw a ship away," Gray completed the sentence. "Okay, so what do you propose? We lure them in?"

"Exactly. It's my understanding that in your last engagement, you performed a hyper jump to save your ship from a self destruct."

"Yes, it was a narrow escape though. I'm not sure I want to tempt fate again."

"My technical crew can show you how to perform a micro jump, one which is designed for quick evasive maneuvers providing you have good coordinates. Our brethren who were destroyed clearly did not anticipate needing a contingency plan or they could've escaped. We'll set our ships for jump in opposite directions, different sides of the planet to keep us apart...and let them commit suicide all alone."

Gray contemplated the situation for a long moment. The plan seemed sound but only if his people pulled off the jump as described. If they made a mistake, they wouldn't get a second chance. Olly was good but could he do it? He'd have to ask him. "I assume you've done this before then."

"In practice," Kale said. "War games but this is no different."

"How do you know our engine is capable of pulling it off? I mean, we had to warm up before."

"The beauty of a micro jump is that it doesn't require full power," Kale replied. "The countdown is soft, meaning you can just hit the button when you're ready. Essentially, we wait until the enemy has already overloaded their power core then we're out of there."

Gray nodded. "Okay, I need to speak to my bridge crew to gauge their confidence level. I'll get back to you shortly."

"Keep the comments about this to private coms when contacting The Font, Captain. I do not want to risk a leak."

"You've got it, Anthar. I'll talk to you soon."

Gray returned to the bridge and leaned against his seat. He contemplated the view screen and the situation at hand. Kale's bold plan made sense, it was the kind of thing he would employ himself. Providing his people could do it, they very well might be able to even the odds again.

"Ladies and gentlemen," Gray said. "I have a proposition for you and it'll take all your skills. Pay attention for a moment and let me tell you what we're going to try. It's a little crazy but then again, we're kind of famous for that."

Chapter 10

Clea leaned against a tree, resting alongside the marines trying to catch their breath. The terrain itself proved far more difficult than anticipated and the traps they encountered along the way made movement slow. After an hour, they were still a couple miles from the facility but at least they didn't encounter any enemy soldiers.

Human armor proved to be highly effective during their romp. One of the men was hit by a trap, a whipping vine pulled tight and held by a trip wire. It lashed him across his chest, tossing him back several feet. Other than a little soreness from the surprise, he came away unscathed.

Another man was set upon by an indigenous insect swarm that covered his body. In order to get them off, he had to jump into a body of water and submerge for a good minute. No one else was bothered by them and Clea discovered he gave off a specific pheromone which attracted the creatures.

Bad luck for him but after cleaning them off, he seemed to be okay.

The humidity was bad enough to cover them in a fine film of moisture. The environmental portion of their armor came into great use, granting them some comfort in the misery of the place. Once they reached the facility, it would be totally controlled with air conditioners and filtration systems but until then, they were stuck trudging through the thick, oppressive atmosphere.

Just before they rested and rehydrated, they were beset upon by one of the local wildlife. Clea caught it on scan a good half minute before it arrived. As the quadruped leaped onto the path, one of the marines fired two shots, both connecting with its head. The beast collapsed to the ground unmoving, and they got a better look at it.

Grayish-green fur covered a muscular body. All four legs ended in fierce claws, which the computer speculated must be for climbing. The fangs were nearly six inches long and the beady eyes were deep set in the head. They passed by, hurrying for the next clearing just in case another such beast might be out in the bush waiting for a chance to strike.

Clea widened her scans and honed them in to get a greater warning if such an animal found them again. Her legs ached as she peered into nothing. She tried to take slow, even breaths, willing her limbs to stop trembling. Daily exercise did not prepare her for this type of activity but she took a moment to be grateful for the discipline to have kept it up.

Without her morning runs, she might've passed out already.

The marines, on the other hand, seemed perfectly fine with their activities. None of them complained nor even lounged during their brief respite. Most of them remained alert, talking quietly amongst themselves. She envied their endurance. These were the true professional soldiers. All the tactics and strategy she learned, all the bureaucratic red tape couldn't compare to the fighting spirit of that unit.

"Listen up!" Hoffner kept his voice down but it still felt like a shout. "Let's get moving, people. Those people are waiting on us." He turned to Clea. "I hope you know how to get in there like you said. We're rapidly approaching their defenses."

Clea nodded. "Once we've got visual on the base, I can send a coded, tight beamed signal. The enemy won't be able to break it. That's our in."

"You're just going to knock?" Jenks asked. "Seems simple enough."

"Can it," Hoffner said. "Okay, let's get there so we can make this phone call. Alsted and McKinney, you're on point to the finish line. Go for it."

Two marines stepped out onto the path and started moving. Clea took up the rear with Hoffner, donating half her attention to the scanner and the other on the path. Nothing came up in their immediate surroundings, no animals to speak of at least but the dense trees around them still garbled some of her readings.

When one of the marines cried out, Clea clenched her fist and rushed forward but Hoffner grabbed her arm, holding her tightly.

"Halt." Hoffner stepped in front of her. "Report!" A gunshot replied. "God damn it!"

"Stop shooting!" Someone yelled. "Christ, you're not that good!"

Hoffner let Clea go and they approached the others. Alsted hung from a vine wrapped around his leg. He writhed around, trying to free himself but it seemed to be moving, countering his motions just as surely as he struggled.

"That's not a trap!" Clea shouted. She squinted, then gestured. A bulb roughly the size of a cargo container undulated and split open, tiny thorns lining the inside. "Shoot that! Right there!"

Hoffner nodded. "You heard the lady, fire!"

Rifles barked, stoccato muzzle flashes erupting in the area. Smelly green goo splattered everywhere, steaming when it hit the ground and trees. Alsted shouted, bending at the waist and hacking at the vine. He gripped his ankle for leverage and began sawing. A high pitch screech burst from the bulb, loud enough to make Clea's ears ring.

"Concentrate your fire!" Hoffner shouted. "Keep it consistent and tear that thing apart!"

The vine began moving Alsted toward the bulb but just before he reached the center, his blade got through. Clea watched him fall and he disappeared into the foliage. Something crunched as he plunged through half a dozen branches and less volatile vines. She winced when the sounds stopped.

A dozen vines floundered in every direction, thrashing violently. "Fall back!" Hoffner shouted, rushing forward. "I'll get Alsted!"

Clea tried to catch him but he slipped her grip, disappearing into the brush. She stood still, unsure whether to fallback or go after the captain. Someone grabbed her and dragged her backwards, moving a safe distance from the vines. "We can't leave them!"

"Trust me," it was Walsh who spoke. "The captain's got this."

She watched, eyes wide as a form paced out of the brush. Captain Hoffner dragged Alsted into the clearing, letting him go as they came close. Some of the green gunk covered his arms and chest. Alsted crouched, catching his breath. "You okay?" Hoffner asked.

"Yes, sir. I'll be fine."

"Good." Hoffner looked at the others. "If you guys are done playing with the local flora, let's get where we're going."

"You were right," Clea muttered. "He...he really did have it."

"Told you," Walsh said. "He's just that kind of guy."

"Yes..." Clea nodded. "He really is..."

***

The defenses loomed ahead, abruptly ending the jungle. The trees gave way to a cleared field, roughly three hundred meters of open ground between the tree line and the high tech facility right in the middle. Clea stepped up to the border, observing the area. Her scanner began beeping.

"I've got the frequency," she said. "I'm reaching out to their control tower."

"Let's make it quick," Hoffner said. "We're looking at a lot of open ground to cover."

Clea programmed her scanner, sending the tight beam to the facility. "This is Vinthari Clea An'Tufal calling Alliance Base, please come in."

"Vinthari?" A female voice crackled in her ear. "Where are you?"

"I'm at the southwestern perimeter near your outer defenses. I'm with a contingency of Earth marines. We're here to extract your researchers and data, over."

The person sighed in relief. "Thank the Gods, Vinthari! Please send your challenge code."

"Incoming." Clea sent her personal authorization to them and turned to Hoffner. "We'll just be another minute."

"By all means, take your time." Hoffner paced away.

"Vinthari, I have verified your identity. Defenses are lowering. Make it quick...we're under pretty heavy assault on the northern border. We might not hold the line for much longer."

"We have a ship ready for departure," Clea replied. "It can get us all out of here um...Listen, my sister is a part of your staff. Vora. Is she...is she okay?"

"Yes, ma'am. Vora An'Tufal is present and uninjured. Please make your way to the facility ASAP. Security will meet you at the door."

Clea nodded. Something popped then hummed for a moment. All at once, electricity filled the air then seemed to suck up into the sky. Silence fell over the area as the defenses dropped. "We're ready to go," she said. "Let's do it, Captain."

"You heard her," Hoffner said. "Double time to the facility. Faster we get there, the faster we can get back to the ship and home. Fall out."

Clea hustled after them, feeling adrenaline rush through her body. She heard explosions not too far off, gunfire echoing through the clearing. The trees and jungle covered it all up before but now, as they drew closer to the real action, she heard the sounds of war in all their terrible glory.

My people are dying out there.

The thought hit her heart like a bullet and she felt sick to her stomach. Those men and women would not die in vain, not while she still drew breath.

Their point men reached the facility first, standing beside the door with their weapons raised. The rest of them drew up and stood to either side while Hoffner advanced close. Before he got within a dozen paces, the door opened and a slight, purple haired girl peeked out, waving them in.

"Quick! We have to seal this up!"

The men filed in and Clea looked around. Her vision adjusted quickly to the low light and her scans picked up over a dozen lifeforms in the base. Power seemed to be at eighty-percent and dropping. Not a good sign. The defenses were responsible for the drain. Her computer suggested they had just over three hours before the entire place would simply shut down.

"Please take us to whoever's in charge," Clea said. "We have a lot of work to do."

"That would be Vora An'Tufal," the girl said. "Please, follow me."

Clea took the lead this time, staying close to the woman. The marines took up a two by two formation and followed, their weapons slung. Hoffner tapped into Clea's communicator, requesting that she set her helmet to private coms. She initiated the request and felt the seal on her helmet close around her throat.

That's not at all frightening.

"Vora's your sister?" Hoffner asked.

"Yes," Clea replied. "Why?"

"That's good news. We should get all the cooperation we need, right?"

Clea hesitated to respond. "Not…necessarily."

"Uh oh…"

"We have a complicated history." Clea sighed. "You'll see."

The gray hallway opened up to an ultramodern command center with consoles lining the walls and a dais in the center. A holographic display of the planet lit up on the ceiling, showing the points of conflict as little red pinpricks. They seemed to be monitoring orbital activity as well with the different ships detailed out enough to determine the make and model of each.

People milled about, some frantically and others more calmly. Clea took off her helmet and advanced into the room with their guide who went straight to a woman with purple-black hair and silver eyes. Her features were older but Clea felt as if she were looking into a mirror ten years in the future.

"Vora." Clea tried to remain placid and calm, as her culture dictated but inside, she wanted nothing more than to hug her older sister. They'd had their differences, they struggled through competition and other foolishness but they still shared blood. For a Kielan, little else mattered in life.

"Clea." Vora turned and nodded once. "Good, they sent someone competent. Do any of these people you've brought know how to copy data from our systems? Backup protocols? Or are they just the type that shoot things."

"We'd like to think we're diverse in our talents," Hoffner said. "Show us what to do and we can help as needed or simply provide security while you handle it. Whichever is easiest."

Vora nodded. "Very well. Clea, I need you to get on that console over there and finish downloading that material. The wipes are taking longer than we anticipated so we might not be able to cleanse the data as thoroughly as we'd like."

"How about destroying it?" Hoffner asked. "Nothing quite eliminates something like blowing it to hell."

"A vulgar Earth term, I'm sure," Vora replied. "But it's possible. The reactor here would vaporize everything. Of course, if we can't get away fast enough, then everything we're doing here wouldn't matter, would it?"

"We have a way out," Hoffner said. "When you get closer to finishing, we'll have them high tail it over and we'll be home free."

Vora directed her attention to the holographic imagery. "From the look of the fighting going on up there, I'd say you're not entirely right about that. After all, the enemy seems to have wiped out several of our ships."

"The two left are more than up to the challenge," Clea said. "Believe us, Vora. You're in good hands."

"Forgive me if I remain skeptical of that, Clea."
Vora scowled. "Just get to work. We don't have a lot of
time to dally. Those animals are on our doorstep and
they have only a small barrier between them and us. The
longer we wait, the better chance we have of being
butchered like animals. I for one would rather be far
away before that can happen."

Vora stormed off, leaving Hoffner next to Clea.

"Not exactly the reunion you were hoping for,
I'm guessing," Hoffner said.

"She's always been like that." Clea moved to the
console and stared down hard, fighting her emotions but
failing. "Since we were young, she never...well...I
mean...it doesn't matter."

"You know, the men gave you a hard time for
hiding your emotions when we saw those men die. I'm
starting to think they were wrong. You cared about them
but you know how to hide it. Your culture taught you,
didn't it."

Clea nodded.

"And your sister excels at it."

"If she feels at all. A danger of hiding one's feelings is no longer having them."

"The fact you're trying not to cry says you didn't succumb to that."

"I'll do my job, Captain. Regardless of how I...well..."

"I didn't say you wouldn't." Hoffner patted her on the shoulder. "But remember this, there's no shame in being hurt by someone like that. You trust her because she's blood, kin. I get it. I can't get along with my brother to save my life but I know he'd have my back if it ever came down to it. I'm not sure you feel the same way."

"I don't...I can't...she's...always the job. And I'm never doing good enough."

"You've been doing great by my book. We're all alive and here. Don't beat yourself up. Even if she doesn't plan on backing your play, we sure as hell will. You're a crew mate and until such time as you decide to leave the Behemoth, that will always be true. Hell, I'd go so far as to say even then, I'd come calling if you needed me."

Clea turned to him, finding a smile. "Thank you, sir. That means more to me than you know."

"I won't always be so sentimental but take it while you can get it. Besides, we've got too much to do to struggle with feelings right now, don't you think? Let's save this data, then our lives. Like your sister, I don't fancy being butchered today."

"I'm on it, sir." Clea returned to her duties with renewed vigor. Yes, Vora may not be the person she wanted her to be and yes, she missed her family. All this time she wondered why she left her relatives behind, she never noticed she'd found a new unit to be part of, an extended family who mostly embraced her.

Chapter 11

Gray pulled Olly and Redding aside to fill them in on the plan. They both waited patiently before speaking, each staring with wide eyes. As he concluded the idea of the microjump, they exchanged a glance as if trying to decide who would ask their questions first. Redding gestured for the tech officer to go.

"I know our system can send the message fast enough," Olly replied. "And I'm sure the coordinates will be fine. I'm just concerned about whether or not the engines can make the necessary pulse to get us moving without blowing up."

"A good concern," Gray replied. "How likely is it that the core won't be able to take the taxation?"

"That's a question for Higgins, I'm afraid." Olly hummed. "But as far as the technical side, I can do it."

"Redding?" Gray turned to her. "What've you got to say?"

"The piloting aspect of a jump is pretty simple. I basically point us in the right direction and hit the button. What you're describing shouldn't be a problem. I can handle it and I know Tim can."

"Okay. I'll ask Higgins about the integrity of his department. Meanwhile, the Crystal Font is going to send you some coordinates. Get them over to Tim and have him plot the hyper jump. Keep the discussion about this to a minimum and get it done. Dismissed."

Olly and Redding both saluted before leaving the room. Gray tapped his com and brought up Chief Engineer Higgins. "I need to ask you a private question. Are you in your office?"

"I will be, hold on." Higgins made him wait a few moments. "Go ahead, Captain."

"We're about to initiate a maneuver we've never attempted. A microjump. Olly can send you down the parameters. I need you to very quickly decide whether or not our systems can handle the load. How soon can you find out?"

"Minutes after getting the tech data," Higgins replied. "If it has energy requirements and time to reach those heights."

"Good, figure out how to make it work. The gamble's a desperate one but it will definitely help. Reach out to Olly for the data right now and call me back."

"Aye, sir. I'll talk to you shortly."

Gray returned to the bridge and sent Adam a text message through the com, detailing what they were doing. His XO smiled when he finished, nodding his approval. Olly worked with Tim, inputting the coordinates. Redding prepared her station for the maneuver. All of them moved with quiet efficiency. It was the most silent the bridge had been in weeks.

Higgins pinged him and he put it on his ear speaker. "Go ahead."

"I've looked at the data, sir and it's more than possible to do what you're asking. I would recommend we throttle up our power just to the point of it being obvious. That way, it won't tax the engines when we suddenly demand full power in a moment's notice."

"Have you calculated what that level should be?"

"Yes, sir and I've already run a simulation. It will work just fine providing Redding doesn't tip our hand by going too fast."

"I'm sure she'll rise to the challenge. Atwell out." Gray turned to the crew. "We're a go on this plan, people." He patched Kale into his private line.

"Yes, Captain?"

"We've confirmed we can do it," Gray said. "And we're making preparations now."

"Excellent." Kale paused. "Our people have coordinated with yours and we're ready as well. We need to not make this very obvious. My plan involves getting close together so it appears we wish to focus our fire on one of their vessels. As we get close, we'll take some random shots, just to get their attention. The tactic has been done by my people before to great effect."

"Interesting...so worst case scenario?"

"We get destroyed by their incoming vessel. If they don't rise to the bait however, then we'll eliminate one of their cruisers."

"I like that optimism." Gray nodded. "Shall be begin?"

"Indeed. I'm patching my pilot to yours. They'll need to stay on tight beam communication throughout."

"Understood."

Let's cast the line and see what happens... Gray leaned back in his seat to observe. It's all on the crews now. Come on you, bastards. Let's play some chicken.

***

Revente sent a broadcast out to the various pilots out at the time. Meagan and her team just finished a quick break and deployed back into the battle zone. The coded message took the computer a moment to decipher. She read it on the screen and her eyes widened. She pinged Mick to see what he thought.

Sounds crazy, came back the text message. We'll have to conserve our resources.

Rudy sent her a message as well. We've made contact with one of the alliance ships and it's still mostly intact. They can accept borders and have stabilized their life support.

"Thank God for small favors," Meagan muttered. Flying escort for the search and rescue proved to be boring in long stretches and chaotic for a few moments. They had contact with the enemy four times, three of which ended with their opponents fragged and the last with a routing where the bad guys ran away.

Her men wanted to pursue but she kept them back, holding them to the task of watching out for the rescuers. As they scoured the wreckage for life pods, they weren't exactly in any position to flee quickly. With all the debris floating around, they couldn't perform any quick maneuvers. The fighters stayed out of the densest junk, allowing them the freedom to remain mobile.

Reports suggested they already found more than fifty people and were able to bring them back to the Crystal Font and Behemoth. Many needed medical attention and the various sick bays were filling up. Now that they had a third ship with nominal power, they could start to relieve the burden by using their facilities but if they couldn't fix their engine for a hyper jump, it wouldn't matter.

We'll have to evac all those people...Christ, what a nightmare.

This new message from the Behemoth added to the stress. With their mobile base hopping away from their current position, any support would be limited. The pilots stuck on board during that attempt would be unable to perform their duties or relieve them, at least for a while. This left them entirely on their own, stranded if something went wrong.

If we were on board and they blow up, we'd be dead anyway. I guess we get the opportunity to take our chances out here...though I'm pretty sure it would just mean a slower death.

Meagan glanced over her shoulder and watched as the Crystal Font and Behemoth headed or their rendezvous. According to Revente's message, they would close in for an attack formation and charge the enemy, attempting to draw them into something desperate. If the plan succeeded, they'd even the odds again. If it partially succeeded, they'd take one down.

And if it failed miserably, both of them would be destroyed.

That's a gamble I doubt I'd take.

Meagan didn't mind some risk but she liked to mitigate it as much as possible. Using the debris field in their last mission or dropping a core bomb, those made sense but this…they basically were using themselves as bait for a massive explosion, one up to the task of taking down multiple alliance capital ships all at once.

Captain Atwell is wily…I hope he's got this one under control.

Part of her didn't believe her people came up with the plan. It was too risky. The Behemoth was the only ship to protect Earth so they tried to be somewhat cautious, or at least treat their home with some respect. Risking her like this…it would've been unheard of back in Sol. Hell, the council would've gone crazy.

Of course, out here with an enemy fleet on the way, they might not really have much choice. It was either take their chances with desperation or hope they could duke it out with the bad guys long enough to achieve their mission.

I miss the time when we thought this would be a milk run.

Pulse cannons fired up and Meagan watched as the Behemoth and Crystal font began firing at the enemy. She held her breath, offering up a silent prayer for fortune in the next ten minutes. Such a precious little amount of time would dictate whether they survived this conflict or lost utterly.

No pressure guys...good luck.

***

The Crystal Font sent over targets for the Behemoth to focus on, critical systems aboard the enemy vessel that would cause the most damage, even if the blows didn't penetrate the shields. Redding entered them into the computer and prepared the cannons. "Ready to fire," she announced. "On your mark, Crystal Font."

"Synchronizing now," a voice piped through the speaker. "And...fire."

Redding hit the trigger, unleashing a swath of energy at maximum range. She kept the throttle at a low level, not tipping their hand as the power levels of the engine hovered well above normal. This allowed them to keep pace with the Font and made the entire situation look like a standard attack run.

"Some hits," Olly announced. "Minimal damage but I think they get the point. They're spreading out."

"Do we have one charging yet?" Captain Atwell asked.

"Negative, sir." Olly tapped at his controls. "The one we're shooting is maintaining position and firing back. His allies are spreading out. They might want to flank us."

"Keep up the barrage, Redding," Adam said. "If they try to close us in, we'll need to redirect fire."

"Aye, sir." Redding kept up the pressure, laying into their opponents with everything they had. Energy splashed off their shields, causing a slight rumble through the hull. With Olly in the tech chair, she felt less stress than when Paul took over. Nothing against the other Ensign but Olly was an honest to God computer prodigy.

"Redirecting power for our shields," Olly said. "I've normalized the output and absorption rates. We should be good for a while."

"Good job," Captain Atwell said. "Any damage on the enemy?"

"The Font did some," Olly said. "I'm reading…significant damage to their forward stabilizers. Nothing too critical unless they want to do any fancy maneuvering."

"Captain," Tim spoke up, "They are altering course, angling thirty degrees."

"Where's that put them?" Adam asked.

"Directing between us and the Font," Tim replied. "They're picking up speed."

Redding glanced over her shoulder and saw Captain Atwell smirk.

"Very good, Mister Collins," Gray said. "Steady as she goes, Redding."

This is definitely going to be the craziest thing I've ever done. Redding felt a surge of adrenaline. Her body tensed up and sweat tickled the back of her neck. The course was laid in and ready to go. Initiating the emergency hyper jump would take a fraction of a second and they'd once again attempt something no other human did before them.

No one can say my job is boring.

Redding hadn't felt so alive since she sat in the cockpit of a fighter years ago, before the first attack. Once she took her post aboard the Behemoth, controlling the massive battleship carried its own rewards but it was rarely as break neck exciting. Especially considering the fact it didn't exactly maneuver on a dime.

"Enemy ship closing to within one hundred thousand kilometers," Tim said. "Closing fast."

"Massive energy surge!" Olly shouted. "They're overloading!"

"Steady as she goes," Captain Atwell said but it wasn't necessary. Redding was in the zone, her body and mind working together in perfect tandem as they moved toward the objective. Now they knew full well the enemy planned their famous sacrifice and very shortly, they'd learn it was a bad idea.

"Crystal Font reports readiness for objective," Olly said. "We'll be going on their mark."

"Very good," Captain Atwell acknowledged. "Initiate countdown with Redding."

"On your screen, Lieutenant Commander," Olly said. "Ready when you are."

"Don't stop firing until the last second," Gray said. "We need them past the point of no return."

"Um, Captain?" Agatha asked. She was the only bridge crew member unaware of the plan. "Shouldn't we be...I don't know...getting out of the way?"

"Don't worry, Ensign," Captain Atwell replied. "I think we've got things well in hand."

The enemy ship stopped firing. Its shields dropped but even firing on it wouldn't stop the inevitable. The thing was going to explode and when it did, any vessels within twenty thousand kilometers would be vaporized. Redding poised her hand, ready to initiate the hyper jump at just the right moment.

"Three…" Olly called out. "Two…One…Now, Redding! Go!"

Redding slammed her hand down, initiating the hyper jump. The ship hummed and rumbled…She felt her senses go dark as the world around her vanished in a second. Time meant nothing until it raced back upon her, making her head pound as if blood rushed from all parts of her body to her brain.

She slumped, fought the weakness and struggled to lift her arms. Muscles refused to respond at first. Her eyes fluttered, battling blurriness. As the world came into focus, she was able to move again and checked her station. All circuits read normal and she had full control of the Behemoth.

"Where are we?" Captain Atwell called out. "Tim?"

"We made our coordinates plus/minus twenty kilometers, sir! A successful jump!"

Olly hooted, his arms over his head. "Can you guys believe it? This old girl has some serious tricks up her sleeve, I swear!"

"Settle down, Olly." Captain Atwell stood. "Get me a reading on the system. What happened?"

"The enemy blew," Olly said. "They went past the point of no return and went straight to hell!"

"The Crystal Font?" Adam asked.

"I've got them on com," Agatha said. "They're reading all systems normal...I wish someone would've told me we were doing that."

"No need to panic you," Redding muttered.

"Course heading, sir?" Tim asked.

"Get us back to the planet, Collins." Captain Atwell clasped his hands behind his back, standing near to Redding's post. "We've got a lot of people to save."

Chapter 12

Clea worked as quickly as she could, downloading massive amounts of data. The files went too quickly past her screen to know what she was looking at but glimpses of the weapon technology drove him the fact she was doing the right thing. They couldn't lose all this information, not after taking so much time to develop it.

The other technicians worked silently around her, every terminal taken up. The marines roamed the area. Every time they heard a noise outside, they poised for action, stiffening at the booms. Such sounds weren't ending any time soon and their nerves would be put to the test for some time.

An especially loud explosion shook the facility and Clea clung to her terminal to maintain her footing.

"Um…what was that?" Jenks asked.

"I'm reading a massive breach," one of the technicians shouted. "They got through the defensive barrier! How did we not hear that? They're on their way in!"

Hoffner sprung into action. "Alright, people you all know what these things are capable of and how dangerous they can be. We won't be taking them in a straight fight, not if we want to walk out of here. They're bigger than us and these hallways are tight enough to give us a slight advantage. Clea?"

"Yes, sir?" Clea stepped forward.

"Are there other parts of this facility your people can download the data from?"

"Yes," Vora spoke up for her. "They're deeper inside."

"Good." Hoffner motioned to his men. "Get these people moving to the next terminal location. Jenks, you're with me."

"What're you going to do?" Vora demanded.

"Destroy these terminals to deny the enemy access to the data," Hoffner said. "While you rush down and get anything else you can."

"These are priceless machines!" Vora protested but Clea put a hand on her shoulder.

"This facility was compromised anyway." Clea tried to keep her voice gentle. "None of it was going to survive."

"We can't just blow it up!"

"That's exactly what we're going to do," Hoffner replied. "And unless you want a close up view of the explosion, I suggest you fall out. Now."

Clea dragged Vora away, forcing the woman to hurry. They got out the door to where the marines waited and jogged down the hall. "Pig headed soldier idiots!"

"Stop it," Clea snapped. "They're here to save your life! Isn't that worth anything?"

"They should be stopping the enemy from taking the facility, not planning to destroy it."

"Part of being a soldier is knowing when to cut your losses," Clea replied. "And quite honestly, we're in that position now."

"It's easy for you to say. You haven't built anything with your life. You're just as you always have been. Ignorant and stubborn."

"Unfair…" An explosion shook the facility and Clea glanced behind her. The control area was destroyed. Whatever Hoffner used in there must've slagged it all. He and Jenks came rushing up behind them.

"We saw the enemy," Hoffner shouted. "Six of them. They stopped to see what they could salvage in there so I think it bought us some time. You'd better move it!"

"There are weapons in the lower area," a technician said. "Some of our experimental ones. It might cut through their armor."

"I'm all for trying new things," Hoffner replied. "Let's grab some of that while the rest of you do your download thing."

Three marines took up the rear. Clea and the rest of the tech team were roughly fifty meters away when she heard gunshots behind them. Glancing back, her heart raced. Did the enemy catch up? Did they need to worry? She pulled her rifle off her shoulder and held it to her chest, preparing for the conflict to come.

"We're not making a stand here," Hoffner said to her, patting her shoulder. "Just keep moving. Our next stop, we'll give them a surprise."

"Right here!" Vora pointed. "This laboratory has enough terminals to make this worth anything."

"It's also next to one of our weapon stores," another person replied, Clea couldn't see which.

Hoffner nodded and took charge. "Walsh, take a guy and see what they've got. Jenks, you and Stebs watch the corridor and raise hell if you see anything coming down there. Hey, are there any other technicians in this facility or is it just you?"

"We're it," Vora said. "The rest of the people are out there fighting."

Hoffner gestured to the soldiers. "You know what that means. If you see something moving, it dies. Don't hesitate. Those things will rip your God damn spine out and none of you has time for that. Got it?"

"Yes sir!" The marines all shouted, making Clea wince.

"Get your shit downloaded," Hoffner barked. "We don't have all day!"

Clea got on a terminal but stepped aside when there wasn't enough room. She paced, feeling useless. A thought dawned on her, something which made her pull out her hand computer. She might not be able to help them download schematics or save any of their work but she could continue the investigation into who tipped off the enemy about their location.

Access to their communications arrays didn't take long and soon she downloaded every outgoing transmission in the past week. Everything from personal calls to official reports went through the satellites but one in particular caught her attention, a hastily scrubbed message with no authorization code.

Odd. We're all far too particular to let such a thing go unnoticed. Who signed off?

The ledger for that day in particular was blank.

Someone erased that too? They didn't do much to cover their tracks though. Perhaps they needed to just buy a little time.

Whoever did it must've thought the enemy would take their facility much quicker than they did. The delayed assault may have given the alliance a chance to discover who sold them out, though it may count for very little. At least they didn't send any data to them. Clea knew now it was all too large to transmit such a distance.

"Contact!" A marine shouted, firing his weapon. They began exchanging fire with someone. This time, the enemy didn't feel like charging into battle as they had on the Behemoth. They took caution. Perhaps there weren't enough of them to make such a push. Either way, Clea aimed her weapon at the door, preparing for the worst of it.

"Sir," Walsh shouted. "Check this bitch out!"

Clea glanced over her shoulder, noting Walsh carrying a massive firearm half her height.

"He says it'll vaporize any organic matter it comes in contact with, leaving the metal walls in tact."

"Then don't just stand here jaw jacking with me," Hoffner pointed, "get down there and shoot!"

Walsh took position by his men, shouting, "fire in the hole!" before depressing the trigger. A lance of green energy danced down the hall and they heard a horrifying scream, something torn of pain and anguish. Clea winced, holding her weapon all the tighter. She took care to leave her finger off the trigger, waiting for the cries to die out before relaxing.

"Is it dead?" One of the marines said. "Are they all dead?"

"Someone sure as hell didn't just ask for another," Walsh said. Another shot rang out. "Nope, they're not all dead!"

"Keep them locked down," Hoffner said. "Hey, techs, you've got less than five minutes. Tie off whatever downloads you've got and we're blowing this room. Where's the next?"

"The next floor down," Vora said. "Nearer the reactor."

Hoffner grinned. "The reactor, huh? Sounds like a good way to cover our escape and bring this place down in the process."

"That's—" Vora started but Clea cut her off.

"It'll be fine, sir but we need to find a way back to the surface."

"There's an access tunnel," one of the techs said. "Leads straight up to the surface on the northwest side opposite the assault."

"Perfect." Hoffner turned to the marines. "Get ready to fall out, men! Hold that corridor at all costs!"

"Shit, I'm hit!" One of the marines flopped on the ground hard and shuffled backward, shoving the ground with his feet. He got three meters before one of his comrades grabbed him by the armor and dragged him to safety. "Armor blow. I think I'm good."

Clea hurried over, running her scanner on him. "It's true. The protective layer stopped the worst of it but there's a hairline fracture on one of his ribs."

"I can handle it."

"Then get back on your feet," Hoffner said, "and move the hell out. Jenks, toss some grenades down there. Make them hesitate to charge."

"Fire in the hole!" Jenks shouted, throwing three grenades down the hall. When they popped, Clea winced and her ears instantly began ringing. The narrow corridor amplified the sound and even with her noise suppression helmet, the volume threatened to deafen her. Hoffner grabbed her and shoved her down the hall.

"Get moving! Now!"

Other technicians ran alongside her and another explosion shook the facility.

"Your thugs destroyed more of our terminals," Vora spoke near her, seeming to appear suddenly. "You've made quite the friends, Clea."

"Do shut up, Vora! These people are saving your life!" Clea glared, her fist clenching involuntarily. "I can't believe you don't see that!"

"You'll never understand anything but your military life, will you?" Vora shook her head. "Perhaps if you'd stop to think for a moment, you'd realize we can lock them down, save them for when the rest of our military shows up and saves us."

"I hate to tarnish your enthusiasm but our military failed to defend this base. They're floating debris up there hoping the Earth ship and one alliance vessel can drive back whatever remains of our enemies." They slowed to take the stairs, moving down swiftly to the next level. Vora directed them to the left.

"You know they'll send more. They won't let this facility fall."

"It'll be a little late if they try now." Clea shook her head. "Anyway, you need to focus on your job so we can survive. I may not understand your world, but you certainly don't get mine and that's precisely where you're at now."

Hoffner pointed at two men. "You two, watch the stairs. Make it a nightmare to get down here. The rest of you provide backup." He turned to one of the techs. "Anymore tricks down here?"

"That rifle should still have some shots left..."

Walsh shrugged. "Hate to say it, but it fried. Didn't you guys have a chance to test it?"

The tech looked perplexed. "We put it through theoretical testing...but that was the prototype."

"It was also heavy as hell," Walsh said. "You know, keep that in mind for the next iteration."

"Next store?" Jenks interrupted. "While we're young."

"This way, sir." A tech motioned and they hustled down the hall.

"Let's hope this works out better," Walsh muttered. "Cause that last one, all mouth, no trousers."

"It fried something," Hoffner said. "Now stay focused and shut it, Walsh. Hey, lead researcher."

"My name is Vora An'Tufal."

"Anyway," Hoffner dragged her aside and Clea felt ashamed at just how much satisfaction she took in her sister's indignant expression. "Why were you freaking out about the reactor? You started to say something."

"Just that if you discharge those weapons down there, you might prematurely detonate something. If it goes off before you want it to, we're all dead. And might I just state, for the record, I protest—"

Hoffner interrupted by raising his hand. "You can put anything you want on the record when someone's got a device recording your concerns. Right now, my only goal is to get you and the data out of here while not leaving anything for the enemy. Retrieve and deny, those are my orders. For the record."

He stepped away and Vora fumed for several moments before returning to a terminal and tapping away. Clea wanted to speak to her again, to try even though they were hip deep in the most dangerous situation of her career. Some piece of her mind, a part warning her about their chances for survival, wanted her to say something in case neither of them made it.

In the end, what does any of it matter? When death takes us, what we said or did not say will not make a difference to us. We will be gone and those left will design their own stories regardless of what we left behind.

Gunfire erupted again, this time at the stairs. Another explosion shook the corridor followed by shouts. They didn't seem to be in pain but rather adrenaline. They called out orders and requests, telling them to take a different position or to find cover. Each of the men out there fighting seemed to be far more prepared than the soldiers who repelled the borders on their last mission.

Perhaps after studying the videos they designed new strategies.

Jenks and the technician returned with two more devices, one a shoulder mounted weapon and the other a thin rod with a curved handle, like a walking stick. One of the marines took the stick, gave it a once over and shrugged. "What the hell is this for? Picking their teeth?"

"He said it'll tear right through armor, man," Jenks replied.

"Why don't I get to try the big one?"

"Because I had to carry it. You get the stick. Come on."

Clea paced over to the hall and watched as they rushed over to the stairs. Jenks aimed the shoulder device up and shouted out, "let's hope this thing doesn't blow up, fire in the hole!"

White light erupted from the back and a ball of red energy discharged up the stairs. When it struck the wall, they heard a series of taps like hail on pavement. It lasted a good thirty seconds before screams accompanied the sound. Something got caught up in the scatter and paid for it.

"Sweet Jesus, that thing is amazing!" Jenks pulled the trigger again and nothing happened. "Are you freakin' kidding me? C'mon, there's no more ammo?"

"We...haven't gotten to full testing yet..." The technician shouted, clearly embarrassed. "And the right mixture for the ammunition hadn't been decided upon."

"Try the stick!" Jenks tossed the weapon. Clea noticed several of the technicians wince when it hit the ground.

The marine stepped closer with the strange, long device and looked it over, unsure what to do. "Aim the pointy end up," a tech said. "Then squeeze the handle and shaft at the same time."

"Well, that sounds dirty," the marine muttered. "Shouldn't I be aiming it at someone?"

"No, it'll seek them out. Trust us! This one's revolutionary."

"Okay..." He aimed, squeezed...and nothing happened. "Um...did I do it wrong?"

"Did you squeeze tight?"

"Like I'm choking someone out." The marine tried again. "Whoa, shit!"

He dropped the weapon just as it began to melt, bits of it seeping into the floor and turning into a hard, flat shell. "Revolutionary?" Jenks turned to the techs. "Revolutionary crap!"

"It shouldn't have done that! But...wait, I think I know why...it was the biokinetic alkaloid mixed with—"

"Dude," Jenks interrupted. "Not the time."

"Alright, enough playtime." Hoffner shouted. "How much longer for data transfer?"

"We should have everything off the computers in another ten minutes," Clea said. "We're making good progress but need some uninterrupted time."

A marine took a grazing shot and cried out. "Well, you may not have it." Hoffner frowned. "Get ready, we're moving to the next station."

"That's in the reactor room," Vora said. "We can't fight there, I just told you that."

"But we can die here," Hoffner said. "So unless you want that to happen, I suggest you pack up your gear and get moving. We'll delay them here with a little surprise. Walsh, rig this area to blow when it's tampered with. They'll think we left in too much of a hurry to take it out."

"Yes, sir."

"The rest of you get on escort duty. I'll be there with you in a few minutes."

Clea stepped forward. "Captain?"

"Not now."

"I just...don't think you should stay behind."

"It'll be find."

"If you die here, what happens to the rest of us?"

"You'll follow the plan and get the hell out of here." Hoffner gestured. "Not get moving. We're not debating this in a conflict zone."

Clea frowned but turned away. She hoped he was right and he had proven to be hard to kill. Still, a commander wasn't supposed to risk themselves and the mission on such small tasks. Humans did things very different than she was used to...and it continued to show in every situation.

Chapter 13

Lieutenant Damon Johns maneuvered his shuttle between two floating pieces of debris, what he guessed must've been crew quarters before the ships blew apart. His scans indicated life forms in a massive chunk of metal and a low emission of energy. He carefully threaded his own craft to the top of the box, deploying powerful magnetics to secure his landing.

Once he made contact, Damon used his thrusters to level out the debris, ensuring it didn't list and crash into something else. By nudging it away from the rest of the damage, he ensured a moderate amount of safety, enough to be considered reasonable risk management. His crew in the back waited for his signal before sealing their docking ring and preparing to cut.

Damon tapped his communicator, sending a tight beam to see if anyone would respond. The last five people they saved had been unconscious and he had no reason to believe these people would be awake either. However, he got an immediate ping back with one word: help. Good God, I wonder how long they've been in there!

He sent the confirmation back to his team, then another communication to those inside steer clear, we have to cut our way in. We'll get you out in a moment. Do you have injured?

The reply came right away many hurt, stabilized but oxygen levels are running low.

"ETA on getting that open?" Damn called back.

"Less than two minutes," Lieutenant Sandra Alton called back. "This stuff's less dense than the others."

"Good, those people in there are awake and running low on oxygen so let's make it as fast as possible. Medical, prep up. They do have wounded."

"What're we going to do with them?" Sandra asked. "It's not like we can just pop back to the Behemoth."

Damon checked the scanners. "They're on their way back, actually. With this lot, we're full up anyway. We'll grab our escort and fly home."

"You make it sound so easy."

"The flying part's easy," Damon replied. "The making it home…that's up in the air."

"Good to know," Sandra grumbled. "One minute."

Damon kept an eye on their position to compensate for any drift. His computer kept the thrusters going in whatever manner was necessary to avoid collision but a few smaller pieces tapped against his shields. They'd already encountered some potential survivors dead because fast moving debris went right through their life pods.

The shields failed on those things and the passengers were completely helpless. Damon shuddered to think about such a fate, drifting in blackness only to be torn apart by unfeeling metal. Sometimes, the dangers of space really bothered him. Much as he loved serving and flying for the military, he had to fight to keep a positive perspective.

"We're through," Sandra announced. "Going in."

"Be gentle," Damon called back. "Those people have been through enough."

"That's our job, Johns," Sandra replied. "Just keep us from blowing up and we'll take care of the rest."

Damon rolled his eyes but patched into his team's com link to listen in. The medical crew called out that they were there to help and not to fire. Probably a good idea considering. He figured the enemy wouldn't bother to board the debris and would've destroyed it but caution couldn't hurt.

He'd never heard of the bad guys taking prisoners.

"We're here to help," Sandra's voice piped through his speaker. "We heard you have wounded."

"One's particularly bad," someone replied. "The rest of us have minor scrapes, bruises and cuts. All stabilized but to ensure survival, we need a real medical bay. Can you help us?"

"Yes," Sandra replied. "Let's make sure your critical is okay to move then we'll board our ship and get out of here. The longer we stay, the better chance this debris will be damaged or worse."

"He's right here," the man replied. "Gil Va'Criz is his name."

"Hi there, Gil," Sandra said. "I need to take a look at your injuries so we can get you out of here. Can you tell me what hurts?"

"Everything…" the weak reply must've been from Gil. "My…my back…my leg…"

"You look like you were in a firefight," Sandra said. "Did you guys have borders?"

"He came from the planet," someone replied. "He claimed to have valuable information to share and was ordered to rendezvous with our battleship...to warn us about a traitor."

"Traitor!" Gil shouted but he paid for it. A coughing fit overtook him and Damon winced. "There's a traitor...in the facility...one of our own..."

"Relax, Mister Va'Criz," Sandra said. "That doesn't matter right now. What's important is we get you somewhere safe." She paused. "Looks like you guys have the blood loss under control. We can move him, carefully, back to the ship."

"I need to tell you..." Gil muttered. "Who...the...betrayer..."

C'mon then, just say it, Damon thought. I'll pass it on to command.

"He's passed out," Sandra said. "Probably mercifully. Let's drop the gravity and we'll be able to bring him up easier. You hear that Damon?"

"Yes," Damon tapped at his controls. "Ours is off."

"Can you do the same?" Sandra asked someone Damon couldn't see. "Also, we need to message command. They need a trauma crew on the hangar deck stat. This guy might not make it too much longer after we get him out of here without immediate attention."

"Understood." Damon sent a coded message to the Behemoth, letting them know they not only had a critically injured patient but that the man may know the identity of the traitor. Considering their situation, discovering the backstabber might make it possible to avoid further enemy surprises. He knew they needed a little luck for a change.

God knows the enemy abused their share.

***

Adam turned to Gray. "Captain, I'm receiving a report from medical. One of our search and rescue shuttles is returning with a critically injured man from the surface."

"Okay?" Gray glanced at him. "What's the significance?"

"He claims to know who betrayed the alliance."

Gray stood up, scowling. "Good. That should certainly help our cause. I wonder what else this guy knows..." He motioned toward Agatha. "Get us a coded frequency to the Crystal Font. Tell them what we've got incoming. They'll definitely want to know which of their people sold them out...and quickly."

"What're we going to do with the knowledge now?" Adam asked. "It's a little late to defend against it."

Gray nodded. "True, but that doesn't matter. They can still do damage and we don't necessarily know where they are or if they have any co-conspirators. If there's a whole faction within the alliance siding with the enemy, then we have a much bigger problem than their fleet heading this way."

"That's how it begins, huh?" Adam shook his head. "We have to start suspecting everyone and everything."

"I'm afraid so." Gray sighed. "Treason tends to be most effective when you can only find one indication of it. After that, you start seeing suspicion in every shadow. Like Othello, everyone's against you and no one can be trusted. It rots an organization to the core."

Adam turned to his tablet for a moment. "They'll rendezvous with us in less than half an hour. Less if we meet them half way."

"Tim, set a course to pick that shuttle up," Gray said. "Redding, engage when ready. We're going to have to move that way anyway to take on the other two ships in the system. I doubt they'll let us pick our people up in peace."

"Probably won't be necessary," Olly said. "If our folks get what they need, they can hop up here and we can jump out without another engagement. So long as we don't look like we're trying to grab the plans, the enemy seems content to let their ground forces do the work…and their pilots. Our fighters are still heavily engaged throughout the system."

"And in need of resupply," Adam added.

"Let's get back to being their mobile base then," Gray said. "And I like your recommendation, Olly. We'll push them when we have to. Right now, we'll hang back and see what happens...and help that poor soul recover from his injuries."

***

Doctor Laura Brand's medical bays were filled with injured from four different vessels. There were so many people, they took over one of the mess halls and a full barracks to offer additional triage units. Anyone who passed a first aid certification helped them stabilize and comfort the afflicted.

Commander Everly sent her a private message. "Doctor, you've got a high value patient about to arrive in desperate need of attention. Can you and a team meet them in the hangar?"

"I'm a little busy, Commander," Laura replied. "We've got a lot of high value patients."

"Not like this," he replied. "He has information we need…it may help with our current efforts."

Laura sighed. "Yes, Max and I will go down there. We're all I can spare at the moment."

"That'll do, Doctor. Thank you."

Priggish military bastard. Laura tapped her tablet hard and found her assistant, Max. "We have to head to the hangar for a high value injured person. Grab your kit and diagnostics. We'll be triaging as we move him to a better location."

"What happened to him?"

"I wasn't told but assume the worst." Laura shook her head. "At least we're doing disaster relief instead of patching up our own soldiers. Better than that last fight, right?"

"I guess we have a better idea of how to take these guys on. The captain learns from his mistakes plus, we've got one of the alliance ships to help. The last time, our backup involved some tech crew and a ship no knew how to fly."

"I didn't think about that," Laura replied. They boarded the elevator and took it down to the hangar level then hurried down the hall. "I wonder how long we'll have to wait."

A voice blared over the speakers, "incoming search and rescue vessel. ETA, five minutes."

"Oh...well, there you go I suppose."

Max smirked. "They read your mind."

"I really hate coming down here." Laura motioned to the energy field protecting them from deep space. She looked out at the stars and shivered. "The fact a quarter inch thick atomized field just isn't enough safety in my opinion."

"Hey, works better than metal," Max replied. "No debris can get through it so you know...no one just dies because we get too close to some rocks."

"You have such a way with words, Max. Thanks..." Laura shook her head. "Just um...try not to cheer me up in the future, okay? I don't think I can handle it."

They saw the ship some distance off, the burners offering it a backlight glow. Men and women moved about the deck, repairing ships and carrying equipment here and there. They'd been far enough away from the action to give the techs a breather to catch up. Now that the Behemoth charged back toward danger, everyone would find themselves busier.

"Search and rescue craft landing in twenty seconds," The tower called out. "Please clear the landing area."

People moved casually out of the way but Laura didn't get it. They were too lax in her opinion. A massive space vessel was about to put down in the middle of their area and they didn't seem to even notice. Sure, they got out of the way but none of them watched as the ship pierced the energy field and began landing procedures.

"This makes me nervous..." Laura muttered.

"Relax, Doc." Max patted her shoulder. "They do this all the time."

"When should we...you know...get closer to it?"

Max motioned with his head. "We can make our way there now. Come on."

They approached as the ship finished it's docking procedures, the landing gear hissing as the hydraulics accepted the weight. A platform dropped, slapping the ground hard enough to make Laura jump. Her ears rang from the clamor of metal striking metal and she frowned. No wonder so many people complain of hearing problems.

"This place is out of control!"

"It's not a petting zoo, doc." Max stopped her from advancing as the medical crew brought down a floating gurney. They saw someone writhing on it, their head moving back and forth as they approached. "I guess that's who we're here for."

"Let's get up there."

Laura turned on her medical scanner. "Download your readings to me," she ordered, taking position near the patient's head. She began her own diagnosis, running the device over his torso. He'd been shot three times and a good half pound of shrapnel seemed to be lodged in his left side. A broken leg added to his list of injuries and considerable blood loss put him in a bad spot.

"Max, call ahead and find out how much blood we've got on hand. He's going to need a transfusion. I'm sending his type to your scanner."

"On it, Ma'am." Max drifted into business mode, no longer giving her a hard time.

"You've done a good job stabilizing him," Laura said, "but he's got a long way to go. We have to get the shrapnel out, find out if there's any ordinance still in his body and do a lot of stitching. Sandra, I want you on this. Between the three of us, we can keep this man alive."

"Ma'am, my team and I are supposed to head back out there."

"This is a high value patient," Laura replied. "This takes priority. Besides, there are over two dozen search and rescue crews in operation right now. I think they can afford to sacrifice one."

"Yes, ma'am." Sandra turned to her team. "I'll see you back aboard as soon as I can."

"Negative," Laura pointed at the rest of her team. "There are plenty of people you can help here. Get down to triage two and pick up the pieces there."

She divided them up then focused on their patient, getting them aboard the elevator. All the readings they gathered gave her plenty of data to start his treatment plan. Unfortunately, their first order of business involved trauma surgery. Infection already started to spread through some of his wounds, likely as a result of the metal stuck in him.

The scanner estimated an hour of surgery if done at a regular pace. Laura guessed the captain wouldn't want to wait that long for whatever information the man had, especially if it meant their survival. She began running simulations to find a quicker way to stabilize him without risking his life.

The computer brought back a variety of options, a few within acceptable risk levels. The percentage chance of his death appeared next to each and she opted for the one in the high eighties. Not perfect, and certainly not to her liking but she understood their needs. Now, to make it happen and ply every ounce of skill she possessed to save him.

Back in the medical bay, they hooked him up to an IV and all the systems required to keep him alive. She washed her hands, put on her gloves and prepped herself mentally for the task ahead. Let's get you through this as quickly as possible, sir. Whatever you've been through, you've more than earned your chance to live.

Chapter 14

Clea's chest ached as they approached the
reactor, her heart hammering so hard it made her ears
ache. Sweat soaked her skin, making the clothes under
her armor incredibly uncomfortable. Those around her
seemed to be in a similar state as the misery of constant
motion worked them over.

Technicians no longer had any more terminals to
download from. What they gathered was all they'd leave
with. Vora complained, stating they were going to lose
years of work but Hoffner didn't care. He didn't even
entertain her comments and shut her down whenever
she tried to speak to him.

"He's a priggish man," Vora said to Clea. "How
do you deal with him?"

"Far more respectfully than you."

They all came to a halt before massive doors and
one of the techs rapidly entered his clearance code to
gain access.

Vora turned to address them all. "Beyond these doors lies the reactor core. If you are truly desperate to destroy half this continent, then we'll have to disengage the failsafes and set the core to blow. Once we've initiated the process, it cannot be stopped so I hope you genuinely have a way off the planet and quick. It will be...thirty minutes."

"Before it blows?" Hoffner asked. "Jesus..."

"Yes, if we're not out of here in twenty five minutes, there's a good chance we'll all be dead. We'll do the math, but it may ignite the atmosphere which, as I'm sure you understand, will mean the end of all life here."

"I see." Hoffner turned to Clea. "Opinion?"

"We don't have a choice about destroying it all," Clea replied. "All the data we didn't get is still in storage banks which can be accessed by anyone with a proper connection. So ultimately, it's a risk we have to take...regardless of how regrettable."

"We're pretty cavalier about a whole planet," Hoffner said. The door opened and they all filed in. "Can this be jammed shut? Buy us some time?"

"I'll make it happen, sir." One of the technicians saluted. "They won't get through without heavy ordinance."

"Don't talk too loudly," Walsh muttered. "They'll probably pull some out of their asses."

"I want three marines to go with a tech and find the passage up. Secure it. The last thing we have time for is a firefight on our way out of this place. The rest of you guard this entrance. Anything starts to happen, you report in. Clea, organize the destruction of the facility. I trust you and Vora can handle it?"

"We're on it." Clea nodded. "Come on, Vora."

"You don't have to give me orders," Vora scowled. "The first one's over here. We have five to take down. When we get to the last one, we should ensure your transport is on the way and everyone knows to fall back or we won't have enough time. I trust your ship is close enough to get here when we emerge?"

Clea nodded. "It'll be a hot extract but we'll make it. I have faith in these people."

"That's where you and I differ." Vora scowled over her shoulder. "They're little more than primates."

"Where does your prejudice come from?" Clea gave her an incredulous look. "I truly don't understand. Our parents did not raise us this way. What's happened? How were you wronged or does it go deeper than all that?"

"I have researched these people and many other races besides," Vora replied. She approached a terminal and started entering a sequence of numbers. "I've seen which are superior and which have failed, which deserve to survive and which should never have raised their heads and looked at the stars. Humanity, your so called assignment, are one such species which we should not have intervened on the behalf of."

"You're so wrong…" Clea shook her head. "I wish you had seen them the way I have but even if I hadn't, I would never condemn an entire species to death. No group has ever warranted every one of them to perish. Every teacher we've ever shared agrees with me so what's your excuse?"

"Our people live and die helping inferior beings." Vora scowled as she moved to the next terminal. "If you saw how they lived, understood their history better and watched their social growth, you'd agree."

"I've lived with them, Vora! Up close and personal on a daily basis. They are flawed, but so are we. Surely, you don't think we're perfect? I can't believe you'd be so foolish or vain." Clea gripped her arm. "Tell me what happened."

Vora shook free. "Nothing happened, little sister." She initiated the next code. "Understanding breeds contempt sometimes and I have developed plenty. Do you think I'm happy to have been stationed in the middle of nowhere researching weapons to fight an enemy we cannot defeat? Do you think this pleases me to see my potential wasted?"

"Wasted?" Clea couldn't believe her ears. "But...Vora...you're a genius. You've done so much with the time you've been given and these developments may save many lives. How could you think, even for a moment, that you have not been useful? Sincerely, I don't understand. I've always looked up to you...admired you despite your sour ways."

"That's not my fault that you have false expectations." Vora finished the next code and turned to the other technicians. "Hold off on the last one of those. We have to arrange our escape after all." She motioned at Clea. "If you wouldn't mind."

"We'll talk about this again." Clea pointed at her. "While we're en route to safe space, you're going to explain to me why you're like this and if I don't like the answer, we're going to keep at it."

"Time's running out, sister." Vora walked away.

"Captain," Clea called to Hoffner, shaking off her frustration. "May I contact the shuttle to come get us?"

Hoffner nodded. "Make it happen. Once they're in the air, get an ETA…we'll throw the switch to give ourselves plenty of time to get to the surface."

"Got it." Clea tapped into the com signal for the shuttle. "Shuttlecraft, this is strike team, do you read?"

"We read, strike team," the pilot replied. "You ready for a ride?"

"Quite. How long before you can get here?"

"ETA of fifteen minutes. Can you hold out?"

"Yes, but we're going to have to make it a hot extraction. This facility is going to explode."

"Understood. Shuttlecraft out."

"They're on their way," Clea shouted. "We need to sound a retreat for the me on the ground, to pick up the other soldiers."

"I'm on it!" A tech replied, smacking a button on his communicator.

Two marines approached, huffing. "We found the ramp leading out. It's a steep incline and running it's going to be a real bitch."

"Okay," Hoffner said. "How long to get to the surface?"

"Ten minutes at a fast pace...but these people, I'd say they're not going to make it in less than fifteen."

"That's cutting it damn close." Hoffner contacted the shuttle and put it on speaker. "Once you get us, how long to break atmo?"

"No more than five minutes, sir."

"Shit." Hoffner took a deep breath. "Once we hit that button, we'll have thirty minutes to get off this rock. That's fifteen to get to the surface, say five to board and another five to get out of here…that is if we don't have a lot of slow pokes. We'll be off the surface with less than five minutes to spare. Pretty damn close."

"We'll make it," Clea said. "I think everyone here's motivated to cut that fifteen minute time frame down."

"Fair enough." Hoffner turned to the rest of the assembled people. "I'm sure you just heard what we're talking about. We've got a real finite window to get out of here alive. If you want to make it and live, you gotta push yourself harder than you ever have before. Getting up that ramp and to the surface is literally the only hope we have. Are you all with me?"

Everyone cheered but Clea felt more fear than excitement. Each person standing around them faced the end of their lives. One false move, one mistake and their time would run out. And that was if the reactor behaved. Overloading devices didn't always follow mathematical protocols. Instability meant unpredictable.

She took a moment to check the long range scans, using the surviving satellites to see what was happening above them. The Behemoth and Crystal Font were quite a ways off and there were only two enemy ships left. Fighters carried on massive battles as they roved the area, taking on threats in every sector of the system's space.

Chaos rages all around us and we're about to make it even louder.

On the surface, she watched her scanner depict another major battle. The alliance forces were being routed and the enemy must've been flooding the front doors already. Something began hammering the door to the reactor chamber, something strong or very angry. Hoffner shouted for the marines to follow him.

"It's time to flip the switch," he called. "We'll make it up by the time the shuttle's here then we're out. Let's move it, people! This is the run of your very lives! Make it count."

Clea took a deep breath and steadied herself for the exertion to come. She already suffered from extreme exhaustion, this particular situation just threatened to make it worse. Pushing her body way past its breaking point hadn't been on her list of activities for the day but now that she was in the thick of it, she summed up a little more energy for the final push.

Whatever it takes, I have to survive. For my family, for the Behemoth and for the alliance. Let's do this, Clea. You can make it.

***

Clea and Hoffner stood together by the entrance to the tunnel leading to the surface. She slung her rifle so it wouldn't encumber her run, but it left her hands empty. Clenching and unclenching, her fists, she battled nerves in her head, struggling with her throbbing heart and the tension forming in her muscles.

"It's just another run," Hoffner said.

"Excuse me?" Clea asked.

"Don't let too much ride on this. It's just a run up an incline. Think about getting through it but not the implications. They don't matter. The only thing you should be worrying about is making it to the surface. Everything else, just put out of your mind. None of it matters."

"Is that how you do your job? How you saved the man from the plant?"

Hoffner shrugged. "I don't know how I do what I do. I just do things and hope for the best. It's not how I advise my soldiers though. As you know, everyone's different. What motivates us or gives us hope, everything is different. The key to surviving in the military, especially on the ground, is discovering what you care about and holding on to it."

Clea smiled. "Thanks…I'll keep that in mind."

Hoffner turned and Clea followed his gaze, looking at the others who gathered around them. Vora continued to wear a sour expression but the rest of her techs appeared relieved. They were getting out of there after all. She believed they cared more about surviving than they did the data.

She wondered if her sister truly wasn't worried about dying. Would she have sacrificed herself to try and keep the facility intact? It made no sense. Whatever conversation they had on their way back to alliance space would be difficult but it had to happen. If they didn't work together, then they'd lose any bond they possessed as sisters.

Not that there was much of one to begin with.

Their relationship, fragile as it may've been, seemed to have taken quite the licking since they parted years before.

"The final failsafe is disengaged!" A young man with blue hair rushed up, panting. "We need to go!"

A loud hum emitted from the reactor as the metal shields began to rise. "Also," Vora added, "We don't want to be in this room when the core is exposed. The radiation is enough to kill."

"Well, we're not staying," Hoffner motioned to the tunnel. "Get moving, guys. Jenks and Walsh, point again."

"Jesus, we're always on point." Walsh jogged into the tunnel with Jenks close behind.

"Everyone else, get on their six and do not stop." Hoffner took a deep breath. "I'll take up the rear and make sure no one falls behind."

"I'll stick with you," Clea said. "You've steered me right so far. I'd rather make sure I don't mess up now."

"Fair enough." The techs filed into the tunnel, moving around them quickly. He glanced at the reactor and gestured. "I don't really want to see that thing in all its glory so let's go."

They started off at a brisk pace, moving onto a heavy incline. One of the techs shouted, "I'm closing the blast door!" which essentially meant they wouldn't be fried as they traveled. Clea tapped at her scanner to bring up a timer based on the energy build up. She frowned at the twenty seven minutes that appeared.

"This might fluctuate," Clea said into her com. "But right now, I'm seeing only twenty seven minutes before detonation."

"Not exactly thirty," Hoffner said. "Let's hope it's like every other time I install software and it jumps up to forty."

"Um...I don't think it works like that, sir."

Hoffner chuckled. "I know, Clea. Stay focused, everyone. The shuttle's incoming and will be here in plenty of time."

Five minutes into the run, Clea's legs began to ache. When she did her run on the treadmill, it adjusted to give her inclines but this seemed entirely different. Carrying equipment, and the weight of impending death, changed the scenario. Plus, and she hadn't thought of it before, the gravity on the planet may be somewhat different than she was used to.

Of course, living on a ship meant planetary gravity always felt a little odd. Earth's in particular made her feel a little on the light side. Another five minutes and her lungs burned. She did her best to ignore it, to concentrate on motion instead of the pain it caused. Those around her, the technicians who were not used to this kind of exertion, seemed to be suffering the most.

They would definitely be pushed to their limits.

Perhaps hustling would cut some of the time down. The fifteen minutes might've been walking. She didn't think to ask and now that they were in motion, it was too late to ask. Of course, how often did they really clock their time? Maybe they were wrong…A chill took the sweat on her neck.

Maybe they were wrong about it only taking fifteen minutes.

That kind of thinking is exactly what Captain Hoffner warned me against.

The shuttle sent a ping to the group and it appeared on her head's up display. They were less than eight minutes out and making good time. Reports indicated the fighting stopped on the surface. Alliance troops fell back and granted the enemy access to the facility. The mainstay of the enemy forces were attacking the front doors, or at least filed inside there.

Clea found some grim satisfaction of what they'd find in there. If they figured it out, they'd likely not be able to get away in time. Yes, the alliance was about to use a valuable asset but the sheer number of victims on the opposing side, the losses they'd endure there…it may not make up for it all but it might make it easier to stomach.

Chapter 15

The Behemoth and Crystal Font prepared to reengage the enemy. As they moved toward the enemy position, Olly kept an eye on various readings throughout the system. He noticed a particularly large surge on the planet, something which made him sit forward suddenly and whack his knee on the console.

"Ouch..."

"What's wrong?" Tim asked, "This too much for you?"

"Shut up, man. I just hit my knee." Olly cleared his throat. "Captain, I've got a strange reading from the surface. If I understand what I'm seeing, it's only going to get worse. Right now, I'd say it's strong enough to wipe out a house but if it keeps going, and I don't see an end to its increase, it might be able to destroy a chunk of the continent."

"Do you have an origin?" Adam asked.

"The facility…" Olly hummed. "It must be their reactor. The Font shared some of their technology with me before we left Earth and it's very possible. They use a renewable energy source but if it's not contained, it's pretty destructive."

"Like our pulse drives." Gray scowled. "Agatha, can you get a message to Hoffner and Clea?"

"I'll try, sir. The interference is pretty intense."

"Get on it. I'm patching into the Crystal Font."

Kale appeared on the screen. "Have your people picked up that energy reading from the planet's surface?" Gray asked. "It looks pretty intense."

"We have." Kale frowned. "Either the reactor of our facility has been damaged or someone has intentionally set it to overload. Regardless, the damage will be catastrophic. We need to get our people off immediately."

"We're trying to reach our people right now," Gray said, " but a more pressing problem is presenting itself. Those two ships have to come down. If they see us going for the surface, they'll be trouble."

"More importantly, I'm sure they have picked up the readings as well." Kale turned away for a moment and nodded. "Yes, they are charging forward…probably not to get their people but in a vain attempt to stop the process. They want that data, they can't afford for it to be destroyed."

"Chances of success?"

"None. That reactor is going to explode." Kale shrugged. "It's just a matter of when that happens."

Gray nodded. "Understood. I've got an idea. How are your planetary satellites powered?"

"Small pulse engines," Kale replied. "Someone from the surface can make course corrections to keep their orbit steady."

Gray smiled.

"What's your thought, Captain?"

"Olly, give me a count of artificial satellites orbiting the world?"

"I'm picking up thirty-three sir. Six were destroyed when the enemy ship committed suicide near the four alliance cruisers."

"That's thirty-three bombs floating around the planet," Gray said. "If we have our pilots grab them, they can hurl them toward the enemy. Meanwhile, our bombers will unleash their own ordinance. All combined, even if we don't take someone down, we'll definitely harass the hell out of them while we put some pulse cannons behind the attack."

"An excellent strategy," Kale agreed. "I will have our people start rounding them up."

"Hold on," Olly said. "I've tapped into the satellite control and am bringing them back around to this side of the planet. That'll make it easier for the pilots...they won't have to fly all the way around to get the back ones. ETA...oh, crap...it'll only be practical to grab around thirteen of them. The rest are too far away. They'd take nearly a half hour even with help from our fastest fighters."

"Can you make them fall?" Adam asked. "Drop them on the enemy forces around the base?"

"Not with any accuracy," Olly said. "Their thrusters are only meant to keep them in orbit and from colliding, not navigating to a specific location on the surface."

"Don't worry about that," Gray said, "it would've been a nice opportunity but we have bigger fish to fry. Get Revente on the line and put our bombers with those satellites. Coordinate with Crystal Font ships to send enough ordinance to distract our enemies. Redding, put us on an attack course. We've got to make something happen now or a lot of people are going to die."

***

Rudy's team had been on standby for the majority of the engagement. When his wing got clearance to launch, he knew they were nearing an endgame. They didn't like to deploy the expensive, larger ships without knowing they'd be able to accomplish their mission. Whatever the captain had planned must be good.

"Rudy," Revente got him on a private channel. "We're trying something a little crazy but it shouldn't be too dangerous for you. Command is sending the planet's artificial satellites against the enemy, using their pulse cores as bombs. You guys are going to send your own ordinance along with them."

"Two for one," Rudy said. "I get it. They can't possibly stop them all, right?"

"Exactly. They might shoot a few down but if you guys unleash everything, we're hoping to see their shields drop."

"Then?"

"Then the Behemoth and Crystal Font swoop in and unload pulse cannons on them." Revente paused. "Just keep back from all the blasts. I want you guys to fire and get out. No heroics. Deploy and run, got it?"

"You take the fun out of living," Rudy joked. "I'm starting to wish I'd taken up with Meagan's wing. She gets to risk her life constantly."

"I'm sure she'll trade places," Revente said. "Get your people in position and wait for my mark."

Rudy repeated the orders to his wing and they headed out to the designated coordinates sent to their computers. Other ships flew around them, the smaller, more agile fighters providing escort. He felt thankful to see them, knowing his own vessel lacked their maneuverability. The bombers carried plenty of armor, enough to withstand a lot of punishment but prolonged engagements meant certain death.

"Hey, Rudy," Meagan's voice crackled in his ear. "I heard you get to actually be useful this time around."

"Glad to see you too, Meagan." Rudy smirked. "Let me guess, you got escort duty?"

"Sort of. My people are going to help hurtle those satellites at the bad guys. Looks like I finally get to know what it feels like to throw bombs around."

"A lot more scary than your little blasters, I assure you."

"We'll see." Meagan flew over him, practically little more than a blur. "See you soon, buddy!"

"Don't take too long!" He called. "We're sitting ducks on this line here."

"I know. We're flying as fast as we can."

Rudy brought them up on his long range scans, putting a camera on it. It zoomed in enough so he could see the first ship launch a tow cable, attaching it to the first satellite. As the pilot gunned his engine, he pulled the makeshift bomb away from orbit and off toward the enemy ships fast approaching.

Jesus, this is going to be closer than anyone thinks. Those guys are really hauling ass!

His own computer warned of the energy surge on the planet's surface, a massive power build up leading to an explosion. Whatever their opponents thought they could do, command disagreed. They said the process was irreversible. Whatever went on down there was going to happen regardless.

"All pilots, this is Panther One," Meagan's voice interrupted his thoughts. "We along with the Tai'Li have attached cables to all available satellites and are moving them into position. Bomber standby to unleash your barrage."

"Just keep out of the way," Rudy said into the com. "We are tying our guidance and detonators to the enemy signal but they're still fast moving projectiles."

"We're pretty good at avoiding those," Panther Two spoke up. "Don't worry about us, just get your big butts back to base safe and sound."

"That was quite the alliteration," Rudy said, "did you come up with it all on your own?"

"Cut the chatter," Revente's voice interrupted. "Focus on the mission. We've got too much at stake for joking around."

Rudy smiled, mostly because he knew Revente too well to think he was actually angry. Stories of his past indicated he'd done some pretty outrageous stuff as a young pilot, up to and including some pretty insane heroics. Because of his results, often the type that won battles, he got promoted. Rudy always thought it was to get him out of a cockpit and into something where his experience would survive.

"Alright, everyone," Meagan said. "We are beginning our attack run. We'll reach maximum velocity then release our cables. When we give you our mark, let them go. We'll get out of the way."

Rudy focused, engaging his computer and preparing to unload every bomb in his payload. He tapped into his wing. "Okay, guys. You know the drill. Enough thrusters to avoid recoil from deploying. No one departs until all bombs are deployed. Fall back together and form up for RTB, got it?"

His wing acknowledged.

The enemy vessels charged toward them. Fighters led the way, providing a screen. If they only launched a few bombs, they might be a problem but they barely provided little more than obstacles in this case. The massive ordinance they planned to send against them wouldn't be a fight, it would be an explosive moment of chaos.

Meagan's wing and the Tai'Li suddenly pulled up, their cables dangling behind as they reeled them in. "Fire, now!" Meagan shouted.

"You heard her!" Rudy yelled. "Go, go, go!"

His ship began to shake as the bombs were deployed, one after another ejecting from his vessel and speeding off toward their target. They rarely did carpet bomb tactics, never fired in such a manner because two or three pieces of ordinance did plenty of damage on their own. If half of what they fired landed, it would cause some serious trouble.

Sixteen bombs each, a grand total of one hundred twenty-eight bombs. As their destructive fleet headed toward their targets, they saw over a hundred glowing turbines driving them onward. "Form up and RTB!" Rudy pulled up, rendezvousing with his wing. "It's on you, Meagan."

"We'll clear a path but we can't do it long...See you soon, Rudy."

***

Meagan felt the cable detach and yanked back on the controls. The satellite flew beneath her, speeding toward the enemy ships. "Fire now!" She shouted to the bombers as her own wing formed up. They needed to address the fighters, clearing them out so the bombs didn't get wasted on smaller targets.

"Get some of those bastards, guys," Meagan called. "Two on one. They like to solo so let them die alone."

Mick took her wing and they closed on their first target, spinning in behind him. The ship tried to climb and bank but her first two shots clipped it's wing, sending it into an uncontrolled dive. It collided with one of his own men and both exploded in a spectacular fashion. They turned, preparing for another engagement.

Blasts erupted around them, flying past the cockpit and nearly taking her out. She made a minor correction, diving enough to avoid the attacks but to keep him on her six. "Get him, Mick. I'm not in the mood for what he's selling."

"On it, boss." Mick flipped around and she saw him blur off as another barrage surrounded her.

"This is getting close, Mick..."

A series of blue colored attacks flew past her, pulse shots from Mick's fighter. Jesus, I'm going to get taken down by friendly fire!

An explosion shook her from behind. For half a moment, she thought she might've been hit. A quick check indicated all systems read normal. "Thank God...And thank you, Mick."

"No problem." The bombs flew past them, wrecking fighters that didn't get out of the way fast enough. Such fast moving weapons cut through anything in their path, ripping them apart without so much as diverting their courses. Quickly, the fighting stopped as enemy fighters tried to get out of the way while the Behemoth shots blew them away.

"Whoa," Meagan shook her head. "We have to get out of here, guys. Fall back. Now!"

They turned toward the Behemoth, burying the throttles as they flew away. Behind them, lights flashed as ships exploded, those who couldn't get out of the way. According to her scanners, they were trying to take out the bombs but there were too many. The satellites helped mask them, making the attack all the more effective.

Her computer began a countdown, a rapidly declining number in the triple digits indicating when they'd reach the minimum safe distance. Five hundred kilometers…four-fifty…three hundred…When the explosion happened behind them, none of those fighters wanted to be in that shockwave.

"Everyone with me?" Meagan tensed up, struggling against the g forces. "Minimum distance approaching."

"I'd like to be a little further," Mick said, "if it's all the same to you."

Meagan smiled despite herself. "Yeah, I'm with you on that…"

They pressed hard, waiting for the inevitable explosion and what may or may not lead to them being tossed off course and killed. Small concerns, huh?

***

"Bombs are away," Olly announced. "We're ready."

"Redding, are you locked on?"

"Yes, sir. We are just within extreme range."

"When those things blow, jam the throttle and unleash on them." Gray turned to the com. "Crystal Font, you on board?"

"We're on it, Behemoth," Kale replied. "Enemy locked, we'll take the one on the left."

The explosions started shortly after, shields flashing on the hulls of the enemy vessels. Redding throttled up, compelling the ship forward. Olly doubled the energy to their forward shields, preparing for the shockwave from the different bombs. With that much ordinance, everything within ten thousand kilometers would feel the blast.

"Fighters have reached minimum range," Olly stated.

"Adam, have Revente order them to get behind the larger vessels and hold there."

Redding turned to the left slightly, opening up with one side of their pulse cannons. The ship rattled from the motion, and as the weapons discharged, the hull hummed. As soon as they discharged their first volley, Redding juked the controls the other way, tilting so they could fire another volley.

Before the first of their pulse blasts reached their targets, the second barrage headed out. The Crystal Font followed suit, their purple energy lancing through the darkness of space. The bombs exploded and the satellites detonated as well. Shields dropped. The enemy's weapons fired but it wouldn't be enough.

As pulse damage riddled their hulls, Olly put the damage on screen. They watched as red began to litter every system. They cracked, bulbs of explosions erupting all over them. The shockwave expanded out in a great dome but dissipated long before it reached their vessels. Their target erupted suddenly, listing to the right then exploding in a spectacular display.

The Crystal Font fared just as well, their weapons piercing straight through the unprotected hulls. A moment passed before it also erupted, shaking a moment before the massive explosion scattered debris in every direction. Gray leaned back in his chair, feeling no small amount of relief as the two went down.

"Thank God," he muttered. "Let's pick up our ships and get back to the surface. We can finally do something at our leisure."

"Captain," Agatha spoke up. "I've got Doctor Brand on the line. She said that the patient is in recovery and may wake up shortly."

"More good news." Gray said. "Is he awake?"

"Patching her through."

"Can the man speak?" Gray asked. "Is he good?"

Laura sounded annoyed, "really, sir? This man barely survived some of the worst trauma I've seen in a long time. He's sleeping."

"Can you wake him up? Even for a moment? We need to know who the traitor is, Doctor. It could be important."

"I can make it happen but you'd better ensure we don't get him up long." Laura paused. "Just ensure you do not take long. I don't want to lose him after everything we've done."

"As long as we find out what he knows, it'll be fine. How long before he's awake?"

"Give me five minutes," Laura replied. "I'll get him up."

"If he tells you who it is, let me know. That'll be plenty."

"Affirmative." Laura cut the channel.

Adam looked over. "Let's hope it works out. Whoever's betraying us can still cause a lot of trouble."

"You're telling me." Gray shook his head. "I can't even imagine who has the nerve to do this. Considering everything else we've got going on, we have to deal with this too? I'm not much of an advocate for the death penalty but in this case, I'd be the first in line to pull the damn trigger."

"Yeah, and believe me, there would be a cue." Adam sighed.

"Um..." Olly cleared his throat. "I hate to be the bearer of bad news..."

"What now?" Adam asked. "What could it possibly be?"

"The enemy fleet has entered the system," Olly said. "I've picked up a massive reading...ships incoming...oh my God! Are you joking?"

"Early? Really? What is it?" Gray asked. "How many?"

"Thirty-six, sir! And they're all incoming."

"ETA?" Adam asked.

"Less than an hour but they're picking up speed..." Olly turned to look at them. "We've got less than sixty minutes to get everyone on board and jump out of here."

Chapter 16

"Just another couple hundred meters!" An exhausted tech gasped out the words. Clea felt a wave of relief that almost overwhelmed her misery but not quite. A tiny surge of strength pushed her on and as she saw the light from outside above her, she practically cried. So damn close!

Her scanner said they had less than fourteen minutes to get off the planet. The ground shook from the building energy, making the entire area feel as though it suffered from natural, seismic activity. Hoffner grabbed her arm and dragged her the last twenty meter and as they emerged into the open air, she took a deep breath and bent at the waist.

"Shuttle will arrive in less than twenty seconds." The pilot's voice filled her helmet. "You've got alliance troops converging on your position. Better ensure they know to keep it orderly. We don't have time to screw around."

"Affirmative," Hoffner called. "Clea, can you take point with the incoming soldiers?"

Clea nodded, unable to respond verbally. She fought to catch her breath and finally stood up straight, looking at the others. A couple of gestures brought them closer and she let out a final gasp before finding her voice.

"Everyone, line up over here. When the soldiers arrive, they'll take up position behind you and you'll all board side by side, two by two. The ship will be taking off quickly but don't stop moving until you reach the back of the cargo bay to ensure there's room for all of us. Any questions?"

Vora stepped forward. "Will we have time to escape the system?"

"Yes," Clea replied. "We're on point to get out of here with plenty of time to spare. Just keep calm and we'll all get through this."

Alliance soldiers began flooding the area in a near panic. They aimed weapons at the marines who did so in kind but Hoffner quickly deescalated the situation with a quick shout. "Hold there! We're getting a ship to take all of you out of here. Lower your weapons and let's work together! I need a perimeter to hold back any enemies who might show up. Got it?"

The soldiers milled about for a moment before one made it clear they lost their CO in a wild exchange of gunfire. Hoffner acknowledged, holding his hands up. "I get it. You five, watch that path there. The rest of you line up for departure. When the tech crew and others board, you'll break off from guard duty and get aboard. Let's move!"

"He has a real command authority," Vora said. "I'm surprised."

Clea scowled at her. "You shouldn't be. Frankly, these people have risked everything to save you and your people. What more do they have to do to earn your respect?"

"They can't." Vora paced away. "So stop trying to sell them as useful beings."

Clea clenched her fist, fighting hard to refrain from punching her sister in the head. The woman had always been infuriating but she took it to new and interesting places now. Perhaps there was no way to bring her to sense. Maybe she had lost any rationality being stuck out there studying weapons so far from home.

Outside the influence of rational people, she became someone else entirely. Clea doubted their family would recognize her anymore.

The shuttle flew by overhead and circled once before landing nearby. The ramp dropped and a voice exploded over the speakers. "Let's move people, this place is not save. We are about to be overrun in less than a minute."

Wow! Clea gestured and shouted, "move it! Get aboard now! Go! Go! Go!"

The people filed on, running two by two. The marines and alliance soldiers began firing, blasting away at the advancing enemy. They broke off, two by two, and rushed back to the shuttle. A turret on the nose helped provide cover, blasting away at the tree line, throwing bodies in every direction.

Hoffner slapped his men on the back, getting them moving. He was the last one to run up the ramp and as it closed, he leaned against it, catching his breath. The ship suddenly climbed and people cried out in alarm as it ascended, the engines belching as it desperately raced to break atmo.

Clea looked at her reading. They had less than two minutes before detonation. The energy readings were off the charts. When the reactor went, it would take the majority of the continent with it. Anyone left down there would be vaporized and anything remaining in the databanks would be lost.

"I hope you're happy," Vora said in her ear. "You've just lost the alliance a major asset."

"You're an idiot," Clea grumbled back. "There was nothing to be saved there. We just barely escaped. You're clearly blind."

"We'll see how the council feels about all this," Vora replied, "when we return home."

"Yes, we most certainly will." Clea turned away and closed her eyes. Her rage with her sister could not overcome a fear that they wouldn't make it to a safe distance before the explosion. As the time counted down on her helmet, she began to quietly pray. She hadn't done so often, but just then…it felt like the right thing to do.

***

"The patient is awake," Laura spoke to Gray through the com. "But he won't be for long. I asked him what he knew…he's talking crazy."

"What do you mean?" Gray asked. "What did he say?"

"He said 'An'Tufal is the traitor'. I don't believe for a second that Clea would betray us."

Gray inhaled to reply but he paused as a man's voice filled the com. "Not Clea..." Pain laced the words as he spoke. "Vora...Vora An'Tufal...she sold us out...sent data...let them know...where...we...were..."

"How's he know?" Gray demanded. "Ask him!"

"Um...how do you know?" Laura sounded uneasy. "What evidence do you have?"

"Recording...recovered just before the attack...at my listening...outpost...I went to report it...when the attackers arrived...they jammed...my...signal..."

"Christ..." Gray rubbed his eyes. "That's why you tried to get into orbit?"

"Yes..." The man coughed. "But right when I boarded the ship, it was hit by that explosion...and I thought my information might die with me. The recording...is here..."

"Send it over, Laura."

"On it."

Gray downloaded the file and watched a video appear on his screen. It showed a woman who looked remarkably like Clea but her expression of bitterness twisted her into something else entirely. He bit his lip as she began to speak, his brow furrowing in thinly veiled rage.

"I am sending you the coordinates," she said, "to one of our most advanced research facilities. The alliance has grown weak. I expect you will purge this universe appropriately and bring about an ideology for the strong. Those who cannot support themselves, those cultures incapable of pushing through their limitations, should be destroyed. My work can help you do that.

"We have two orbiting vessels and a number of ground forces. Be aware of our other defenses as well. They are listed below."

Gray clenched his fist as he listened to her give them everything they needed to annihilate the planet. He shook his head and stood, slapping the com. "Let him rest, Laura. he's done his part. Agatha, patch me through to Hoffner and Clea, ASAP. Priority one."

"Working on it, sir. The interference from that energy surge is playing havoc with outbound communications."

"Cut through it, this is important."

"Establishing a weak connection now..."

"Thanks, Hoffner? Clea? This is Gray, can you hear me?"

***

Clea put her hand to the side of her helmet, pressing it into her ear. "Captain? I can hear you, this is Clea...your signal is very weak."

"Pay close attention to what I'm about to tell you," Gray said. "We've identified the traitor."

"Good," Hoffner replied. "Where is the bastard?"

"With you, I assume," Gray said. "It's Vora An'Tufal. We have a recording from her that she sent to the enemy. It's pretty damning. In fact, I'm sending it over."

Clea watched the video in silence, her back stiffening. From beginning to end, she didn't move an inch. Every fiber of her being, every nerve ending and sensation went numb. Her blood ran cold and sweat instantly dried on her back. An energy filled her muscles, replacing exhaustion with honest rage.

Hoffner grunted. "That bitch! Clea, are you near her?"

Clea didn't respond. She turned to her sister, eyes narrow and glistening with unshed tears. The faceplate of her helmet hid the emotions playing out openly on her face, in direct defiance of everything she'd ever learned about maintaining discipline. Third hand betrayal upset her, the very idea anyone would turn on them sickened her. But this...

A thousand memories flooded Clea's mind going back to when she was a child. They ran together, threw rocks in the pond near their house, received the same tutoring for a time and played games with friends. Their mother taught them to cook and Vora fussed about getting messy. Her sister's eyes never lit up so much as when she indulged her passion for science.

So why would you have done this?

Clea couldn't confront her on the shuttle, not in front of all those people. Not only would they likely beat her to death but they didn't need to hear whatever she had to say. There was no defense for her actions, no justification which anyone would accept. This situation, as it stood, damned Vora completely.

My sister...

A tear finally fell, streaking her cheek before absorbing into her collar. The armor felt insanely restrictive, biting into her skin and irritating her. She wanted nothing more than to tear it off and throw it on the ground, to remove the offensive garment but people crowded around her, making too much movement impossible.

"Clea?" Hoffner had been speaking to her for a good several minutes and finally got through her thoughts. "Hey, talk to me."

"I'm here, Captain." Clea tried to make her voice sound distant but her words trembled and she felt like she was falling into a great pit. "I'm here."

"We can't do anything here…"

"I know." Clea replied. "But when we board the Behemoth, I'll take her aside. You can have some marines follow so we can arrest her properly. However, I must talk to her."

"Is that a good idea?" Gray's voice filled her helmet. "Clea, you don't have to talk to her. Leave it to the MPs. They can put her in lockup and question her later. You shouldn't—"

"She's a blood relative, Captain," Clea interrupted. "One I grew up with. I will understand her motivation before she is sentenced. Whatever happens to her after, that's her business but at least right now, she'll explain it to me. After all, I'll be responsible for explaining it to our parents…to making our family understand. I have to mitigate the damage to our family as well.

"Vora has much to answer for. Her betrayal is merely the most important."

"Okay," Gray conceded. "Hoffner, ensure you pick a couple of men who are discreet. No vigilante nonsense, got it?"

"Yes, sir."

"She may know more about the enemy," Gray said, "and if so, then this might not be a complete loss."

"I hope you're right," Clea said. "Because if you're not...then she's thrown away her life for nothing."

"I'm sorry, Clea." Gray sighed. "More than you know."

"So am I, Captain." Clea clenched her fists tightly. "So am I."

***

As the shuttle broke atmosphere, a massive explosion rocked the continent where the research facility had been. The flash of light bathed the ship for a brief moment before dying down and falling silent. When they looked again, a massive crater formed over a twenty-thousand kilometer radius. Nothing could've survived the blast.

The facility, and any secrets it may've still had, were quite gone.

They docked with the Behemoth only a few minutes later. As the ramp dropped, medical personnel welcomed the people aboard and escorted them to one of the triage centers. Clea waited patiently for her turn to leave, staying close to Vora. Her sister continued to look sour, not even an ounce of gratitude filling her angular face.

Would you have rather died down there? Clea began to wonder. There was a chance, however slim, that her sister knew she'd done something wrong. Perhaps she hoped to die when the enemy arrived, sacrificing herself for this mad ideal of inferior races and those who didn't deserve to live.

Who made you one of the gods?

The ship emptied and Vora followed the last survivors off the ship with Clea close behind. Two marines followed as she tapped her sister on the arm. "We need to go this way." She gestured with her head off to the left, down a hall toward the brig.

"Why aren't we going with them?"

Clea hesitated for only a moment. "Because we're not hurt. Come on."

Vora shrugged and walked along with her sister, moving into the privacy of the hall. Clea stopped her there with a touch to her arm. "Do you remember..." She swallowed back emotion, struggling for a moment to maintain her composure. It took a moment but she finally mastered herself and continued. "Do you remember the An'Vell plantation?"

"Of course." Vora nodded. "They grew those amazing filans."

"We snuck in there and gorged ourselves during the hot months."

Vora finally smiled, the first positive expression she'd shown since they met up again on the planet. "Yes...it made us sick for days."

"Thank God." Clea took her helmet off and set it on the ground. "I had to know if you'd lost all feeling. I'm glad to see you haven't."

"What're you talking about?" Vora tilted her head, looking confused. "Clea..."

"I know what you did." Clea held up her computer and showed her the video. Vora watched, standing up straighter the moment she saw her own face. The words didn't seem to move her but she didn't look away until the video finished.

"I thought I'd deleted all trace of my indiscretion."

"Is that what you call high treason?" Clea asked. "Indiscretion? As if you've done nothing more than annoy a person?"

"I followed my conscience."

Clea shook her head. "No, no…no, you did not. If your conscience told you to do this, then you wouldn't have tried to get away with it. You wouldn't have cared. Unless you thought you might do more damage to your own people."

"We've grown decadent—"

"You haven't been home in a while." Clea shook her head. "Are we amongst those species which don't deserve to live? Mother? Father? Our brother?"

Clea felt a surge of anger threatening to overtake her and she swallowed it back, fighting with every fiber of her being to contain it.

"The enemy has won." Vora shrugged. "There's no use fighting them. They have devoted all their resources to battle, to destroying us."

"How do you know that? What did you discover?"

"It doesn't matter..."

Clea grabbed her by the shirt and slammed her into the wall, raising her voice. "It matters, Vora! It matters to all the people who died today out in space! Our culture depends on what we do here and now, what you tell me and what you give up. So don't try to hide behind some nihilistic nonsense! Tell me what you found!"

Vora looked away, shame filling her features. "Our research into enemy technology led me to stumble upon one of their archives. After a battle, our ships recovered more of their data core than ever before. I personally studied it, eager to learn more about those who would kill us. I thought I might be able to provide context, a weakness in their social structure we could exploit…"

"But?" Clea prompted. "What was it?"

"When we made contact with those people, they were content to their colonies and home world. Their social structure, their caste system, was rigid and well defined. Even before they had a cause, their religious zealotry bound them together. Their morals were unshakable and their ideologies uncompromising.

"When we met them, with our liberal attitude toward sharing knowledge...our concept of freedom and individuality...it offended them. We could not treat with them because they had no interest in what we had to offer. They didn't appear technologically savvy but what we didn't know was how well they guarded the secrets they'd uncovered in their colonial expansion.

"They have some sort of manufacturing planet capable of churning out equipment, ships and fighters, some sort of...of precursor tech we can only imagine. For every two ships we destroy, they can produce five and they do so with resources claimed from other worlds nearby, strip mined to fuel their jihad.

"Make no mistake, they want us dead due to religious and ideological differences. They are not interested in a cease fire or any kind of peace. Their only goal is to annihilate any culture which defies the tenets of their race. We represent the largest threat to their goals. The longer we struggle, the more we prolong the inevitable."

Clea stared at her with wide eyes. The revelation she'd been presented with, the story Vora carried with her, made her stomach turn. "So you just gave up? Decided we weren't worth fighting for? How could you have so little respect for your own life? What happened to your self preservation? Why didn't this compel you forward, making you search harder for the technology we needed to win this war?"

"Because you are not listening!" Vora shouted. "There is no victory here!"

Clea closed in so their noses were touching and their eyes were inches apart. She whispered harshly. "I for one would rather fight to my dying breath standing between my enemies and my family than to roll over and surrender to cowardice."

Vora opened her mouth to respond but Clea's scowl stopped her.

"You cannot defend yourself from this. You can't make amends. You can't escape the judgement you've requested. In attempting to damn our entire race, you've merely thrown all your potential away. Giving up never helps anything, Vora. Don't you remember that simple lesson? Our father made it quite clear."

"He didn't face these odds."

Clea shook her head. "He did state any odds." She pulled her sister close, embracing her tightly. She recited their traditional statement for a condemned prisoner, her eyes burning with tears. "I hold the remnants of Vora An'Tufal in my arms. When I release her, she will be known only as Vora. Her ties to family and tradition will be cut. Only the individual will remain and she will pay for what she has done."

The gravity of it must've sunk in. Vora returned the hug and began to cry, burying her face in her sister's hair. "I'm sorry, Clea..."

"I wish I could believe you." Clea fought hard to let go but couldn't immediately. "I wish you would've thought about all of us first. I'll miss you. The memories I'll cherish will be those of our youth. The other actions are those of another and that's the person I'll see punished."

Vora nodded, unable to speak through her weeping.

As Clea stepped back, she directed the soldiers forward. "Take Vora to a cell. I'll accompany you."

"Yes, ma'am." She recognized the men as Jenks and Walsh. Their familiar presence gave her some strength. Walsh smiled at her, offering a sympathetic expression before bringing their prisoner down the hall and to the brig.

So ends the hunt for our traitor...and the life of my sister.

Clea saw her locked up and headed for the bridge. They still needed to get out of the system if any of this was to matter.

Chapter 17

Gray stood behind Redding, watching the view screen. Olly put up the position of the enemy fleet and it was approaching fast. They know the facilities gone, they have to. They must assume we got everything out of there. The thought worried him. Would they try to blow them out of the sky or commandeer the ships to get at their cargo?

The traitor situation made his heart sick for Clea. He knew what family meant to the woman, how much it meant to their culture. Having her own sister do such a thing must've been quite the blow. He'd received the report that Vora An'Tufal was locked up in the brig. He wondered if he'd see his liaison any time soon.

Technicians worked to backup the data recovered at the facility. Tech crews assisted with Paul on lead. He'd been working in the computer labs when those people arrived and broke off to ensure everything they saved got some redundancy. Olly didn't have the bandwidth to coordinate any of that, especially considering their current situation.

The Crystal Font came closer to them and they allowed visiting fighters to return home. Gray turned to Olly when the last ship boarded. "Are we ready to jump out of here?"

"The engines have been charging for almost ten minutes," Olly replied. "I'm not sure what's taking so long."

Gray gestured to Agatha. "Patch in Higgins."

"He's on the line, sir."

"Higgins, what's going on? How long to jump?"

"We're working on it," Higgins replied. "That microjump messed with the charging stations. Our sensors said they were working fine but when Olly called down to ask what happened, I found they were trickle charging."

Gray rubbed his eyes. "Is the problem corrected?"

"It is now…"

"How long before we can jump, Higgins?"

"Five minutes, sir."

"And how long before the enemy fleet gets here?" Gray looked toward Tim.

Tim replied, "at present speed, they should have a firing solution in less than eight minutes."

"Not much room for error," Adam said.

"Plot a course away," Gray said. "Redding, turn us around. Get us moving at top speed. Buy the drive some time to charge."

The navigator and pilot went to work. Gray brought the Crystal Font online. "Kale, we've got a problem."

"We were just about to recommend a jump...where are you going?"

"Our pulse drive isn't charged up. Something happened when we did the micro. We're going to put some distance between us and that fleet long enough to get the drives ready. It'll be about five minutes."

Kale hummed. "I see."

"You guys are welcome to take off. I'm sure your ship's ready to go."

"We can't leave you here," Kale replied. "Not with the cargo you carry. The data, the traitor...between the two of us, we are the expendable."

"Listen to me," Gray said firmly. "No one is expendable, okay? No one." Clea came on the bridge and stopped abruptly. Gray made eye contact with her and frowned. She paced closer.

"I'm not saying I wish to die," Kale said. "Nor do I necessarily plan to. I have some tricks up my sleeve still and I should be able to get out of here before they dust my ship. However, you need time and I can buy it for you. Keep your throttle at maximum and jump out of here. We're sending you some coordinates. From there, you can jump back to Earth."

"What about you?" Gray asked. "What'll you do?"

"Go in another direction…a roundabout way to get home." Kale smiled. "They'll be far more interested in us than you in a few moments so we'll have to take the long way back."

"I see." Gray shook his head. "I don't like it, Kale. We've been through a lot together. I really wanted to see this through to the end."

"And we will," Kale assured, "just in different parts of the galaxy. I look forward to our next meeting, Captain Atwell." He pressed his hand to his chest and bowed his head.

Gray nodded once and saluted the man. "Likewise, Anthar Ru'Xin."

"Crystal Font out."

"They're going to try to run," Clea said. "But how will that help us?"

Agatha turned to them. "The Crystal Font has sent us a message. They offer thanks for returning the data from the facility and wish us a speedy trip back to...to Xion Six? Where's that?"

Clea smiled sadly. "That's a planet on the outskirts of our space...a deserted world. If you check the chart, it's in the opposite direction of Earth."

"Clever," Adam said. "That guy's good."

"I hope he makes it," Gray looked at Olly. "You tell me when those engines are ready for us to get the hell out of here, okay?"

"Yes, sir." Olly put the charging meter up on the main screen.

"Are you okay?" Gray asked Clea and she nodded once. "You don't have to be here for this. I know you've been through a lot."

"Captain, in the next several minutes, we very well may be dead," Clea said. "I'd rather do that on the bridge, at my post and not in my bed, hoping."

"Very well." Gray motioned for her seat. "Your station, please Vinthari."

"Thank you, sir." Clea sat down and leaned back, looking over the reports. She frowned at the energy build up in the engines and shook her head. "This is wrong."

"What is?" Gray asked.

"The engines..." Clea stood and joined Olly at his terminal. "Bring up the power relay six."

He tapped his screen and they saw a three dimensional schematic of it. "Indicate energy flow." Olly did so and they saw a strange pulse on the wave meter. Every ten seconds, something surged. "That's bad."

"What is that?" Olly asked. "I've never seen anything but regulated power down there before."

"Whatever happened to the rechargers has them cycling additional energy unevenly. While it will still charge up the engine, we're relying on a continuous flow so we can do it again any time this year." Clea picked up her own tablet, her fingers flying over the controls. "This has to be fixed before we jump or we'll be stuck wherever we show up."

"Thank God you caught it," Adam said. "What brought it up?"

"Our top report is from Higgins indicating the rechargers malfunctioned during the microjump. I checked their output and noticed the surge." Clea glanced at him. "After helping to implement those drives, I know precisely what they are supposed to do and how they do it."

"Can you fix it from here?" Gray asked.

"No, I'm sending the formula down to engineering now and will guide them through the process on the com. There's no time to run all the way down there."

"No, there's not," Tim said. "The enemy is now pursuing the Crystal Font. They're moving around the other side of the planet, out of visual range. A small contingency of the fleet has decided to pursue us."

"How close are they?"

"Outside extreme range but closing." Tim shook his head. "Can we get any more speed, Redding?"

"Not without tapping into power we're storing to jump out of here."

"We'll make it," Clea said. "Believe me, I will ensure we do."

"What would've happened if we tried to jump?" Adam asked.

"Worst case scenario, the ship would've exploded," Clea said. Adam, Tim and Olly all gave her an incredulous look. She cleared her throat. "The more likely scenario involved getting stranded where we emerged."

"Well, I'm glad there's a narrow range of possibilities," Tim snarked.

Gray watched over Clea's shoulder as she rapidly typed up a mathematical formula for the engineering crew to implement. She hit send then pulled on her headset, connecting with Higgins. Gray tapped into the line so he could listen along, gathering data straight from the source.

"The key to our problem lies in the computer's ability to regulate the power," Clea said. "There are multiple possibilities that could be causing this error: the computer code may've become corrupted during the microjump, one of the relays may be damaged or the charging devices are producing inconsistent power."

"I think we can hold off on root cause analysis," Higgins replied. "What am I doing with this formula?"

"I've already decompiled the code," Clea said. "Insert that data between lines thirty-six hundred and thirty-seven hundred. There's a solid break there. This new formula I designed will override the others and clean up the power going to the engines. Instead of pulses, the engine will only accept it at a rate I've indicated."

"And you're sure the rate you've created will be correct?" Higgins sounded doubtful and Gray shared some of his concern. However, few people knew the technology aboard the Behemoth as well as Clea.

"I am one hundred percent positive," Clea replied. "Install the code, Higgins. We're running out of time to recompile it."

"God damn son of a…"

Gray ignored Higgins quiet rant and turned to Clea. "Do you think Olly can help get the code back up and operational quickly?"

"Not any faster than I have," Clea said. "As soon as he puts in the formula, I'll have it ready to go in less than a minute. I debugged it through a simulation and it returned positive results. Ultimately, we don't have a choice in the matter, sir. There's no time for better than my makeshift solution."

"Enemy fleet is firing at the Crystal Font," Olly said. "They are on the other side of the system now so we've totally lost visual."

"How're they doing?" Adam asked. "Any damage?"

"So far, they seem to have survived the initial onslaught. Wait…" Olly paused. "They sent me a message. They're waiting for us to jump before they leave!"

"God damn it." Gray slapped his console. "Clea…"

"Higgins is doing his best sir."

"I'm done!" Higgins shouted. "The code is placed!"

Clea took a look and hit the button to recompile. She remained motionless throughout the process as a percentile bar climbed toward one-hundred. It stalled at sixty, making Gray's heart jump in his chest then proceeded again up to eighty. By the time it hit a hundred, he thought he would have a heart attack.

"Are we good?" Gray asked, waving his hand as if he might hurry her up.

"I have to check it now, sir," Clea replied. "It'll be a moment."

"We don't have a moment!" Tim called back. "Enemy is approaching extreme range for weapons!"

Clea worked quickly but did not respond to the others. She brought up the system and performed a diagnostic check. A moment later, Higgins received the signal and did his check, backing up her opinion. An energy blast flew past the ship, narrowly missing. Olly called out the proximity as less than one hundred kilometers.

"Aren't they accurate," Adam turned to Redding. "What will evasive do to us?"

"Slow us down, sir," Redding replied. "I'm on as full a sprint as I can without compromising the integrity of the ship."

"Clea, they are going to make any jump pointless soon," Gray said. "I appreciate your risk analysis but we really need to make some headway on this trip. Now!"

"Readings are normal," Clea replied. "All systems read functional…the new formula is doing its job. Engines are only accepting the proper amount of energy. It worked."

"Thank God!" Adam turned to Olly. "Are we ready to go?"

"Engines show they are full up." Olly nodded. "I'd say we can punch it."

"Agatha," Gray said, "send a final message to the Crystal Font. Tell them we're jumping out and Godspeed. We'll see them again…one way or another."

Agatha sent it as a tight beam text message, typing swiftly. "Message away, sir!"

An explosion brightened the other side of the planet, a massive surge of light which made the world between them into a silhouette. Gray scowled but gestured to Redding. "Get us out of here. Now."

Redding nodded once, slapping the controls to initiate the jump. Another series of beams nearly collided with them, one sizzling the shields. The strange weightlessness fell over them and a moment later, the ship faded from existence, leaving behind the system and the enemy fleet.

Gray found himself lost, stuck in a foggy dream. He saw a field of grass fading into a blue sky horizon. Off to the right, mountains climbed toward the heavens and on the left, a distant sea licked the shore. Wind caressed his ears, drowning out any sounds or distractions around him.

All at once, the ship reappeared and his senses instantly returned, causing a flash of pain in his skull. Gray stumbled backward and flopped into his seat, pressing his fingers tightly to his forehead. "That wasn't pleasant at all…" he muttered, "anyone know what happened?"

"Normal jump, sir," Clea replied. "All systems report operational. Engines are charging and should be prepared in thirty minutes."

"Good…" Gray leaned forward, his elbows on his knees. "We made it…"

"Again," Adam added. "These close calls are getting a little old."

"Space combat isn't cut and dry," Clea answered. "It can be unpredictable…just as most major battles. Right, Captain?"

Gray nodded. "Mostly true, yes. But I wouldn't mind a straightforward engagement…or even a mission to be what we assume. Redding, let's hold position here until we're ready to go. Have all departments report in. Olly, did you get any readings just before we hopped out? Was that explosion the Crystal Font?"

"I'm not able to tell, sir." Olly shook his head. "I'm afraid we left right when I might've gotten something back. Whatever it was made quite the wave though. The energy readings were enormous."

"Might not have been an explosion," Clea said. "It could've been an emergency jump."

"That was a pretty spectacular display for a jump..." Adam smirked. "Not...that I really know what a jump looks like...per se."

"There you have it." Gray looked around and took a deep breath. "You've all done outstanding work here. Every one of you vastly exceeded my expectations. We're all alive because of your quick thinking, skillful execution of your duties and hard work. I commend you all. Thank you."

Redding, Tim and Olly each stood, turned and saluted. Gray and Adam stood and returned the gesture. They remained for a good minute before relaxing and returning to their stations. Their successful escape meant a great deal to the alliance and to Earth. All the technology they saved, and the lives accompanying it was a powerful victory, even if they lost the facility that housed both.

Gray thought about the various losses, the multiple alliance ships in particular. Those men and women gave their lives protecting that place. Each of them suffered the ultimate sacrifice. It honored the Behemoth to be able to carry on for them, to give their end a meaning. Had they lost their own people on the surface or been destroyed, the defeat would've left the alliance staggering.

Protocol Seven didn't work the way they'd hoped but Olly already found some ways to improve upon it. With the help of the alliance technicians, they may find the necessary breakthrough to employ it. Combined with all the other discoveries, Gray hoped they would develop a new advantage to overcome their foes.

Earth command would have a great deal to say when they returned home. Their work proved exemplary and they returned relatively undamaged. The others took the brunt but their improved understanding of the enemy, and help from Kale's Crystal Font, meant they were able to come back in operational order.

Kale may've been a new Anthar for the Alliance but he knew his stuff. Without him, Gray figured they may not have come away unscathed or at all for that matter. Superior tactics saved them. It dawned on him that with such a vast fleet, the enemy could not employ brilliant commanders to each. That was a stunning oversight to take advantage of.

Maybe dramatic technology wouldn't win the day. Advances in their overall designs and weapons would help but didn't necessarily represent the silver bullet to end the war. Tactics, ingenuity, free will and self preservation, those seemed to be the values to stand upon for victory. So far, humanity survived multiple engagements with these invaders and each time came from raw desire.

Reports filtered up from the various departments, detailing the state of the ship. Some reported minor damage from the various maneuvers, others had injuries which were being tended to in the various triage and sickbays. All around, they came away fairly clean. Nothing they encountered would be missed in routine maintenance.

Damage caused by the microjump concerned Gray. They would definitely perform a full diagnostic of the system to determine what went wrong and how to correct the problem. Such a tactic seemed to be part and parcel to the alliance handbook. He didn't want to be hamstrung by losing a tool at his disposal.

Perhaps Clea would be able to help. Poor Clea. The situation with her sister made his heart hurt. Now that they had a moment to take a breath, he wanted to speak to her in private, to see if she needed to talk before they returned to Earth. They'd jump in near Saturn and have hours of flight time before arriving home.

Once they all had some downtime and got underway, Gray knew he'd have an opportunity to speak and relax. Everyone on board deserved some R&R, especially the soldiers and pilots who pulled double duty and risked their lives throughout the operation. He hoped the council wouldn't send them immediately back out on another mission. They needed at least a couple days.

If for no other reason, they needed to work out the glitch from the engines. While that may not take long, Gray knew it would give the majority of the personnel the time they needed to take a deep breath. It may not be much but considering all they'd been through, it would be worth it.

He sure wouldn't balk at a decent meal and a night's rest.

Epilogue

Clea approached Gray's cabin and knocked on the door. She stood tall in her uniform, hands clasped behind her back as she waited to be summoned. Once they jumped back to Earth space, key personnel retired to their quarters to clean up and eat. After a shower, she felt like a new woman but the process wouldn't be complete without a reasonable rest period.

"Come in," Gray called and she stepped inside. He sat at the table with a cup of coffee, peering down at an old book. She stood in front of his table, head held high. "Sit down, Clea. This isn't a formal summons."

She relaxed a little and sat across from him, in the same chair she'd occupied dozens of times while they played chess.

"I read your assessment of Vora," Gray said. "The conversation you had...I just...I wanted to say I'm sorry."

"Thank you, Captain." Clea bit the inside her cheek to maintain a neutral expression. She nearly cried in the shower but fought it back. If she wouldn't do it alone, she sure didn't plan to do so in front of Gray, regardless of how gentle he might be. "It was...an unfortunate circumstance, one I will have a hard time explaining to my family."

Gray smiled but it seemed to be a sad one. "Clea...you don't have to lock your feeling away. You've got them and this situation sure warrants your ability to let them go."

"It won't help, Gray. Vora made her decision and now she has to live with it...for so long as the alliance allows her to." Clea turned away, looking out the porthole at the stars. "I didn't think anyone I personally knew had the capacity to turn on their own people. The revelation has caused me more pain than I can relate."

"I understand...such things are never pleasant. Our own history has a number of such incidents and they never go over well. They have far reaching ramifications which may not be realized for weeks, months or even years." Gray sipped his drink. "But I hope you're not doubting anything as a result of this."

"If anything, my resolve has been strengthened," Clea replied. "This enemy corrupted my sister with their violent, horrifying ideology. I refuse to be broken because she lost her way. I refuse."

"Good." Gray leaned forward and patted her arm. "You're a stunning officer and a woman of integrity. Never forget it."

"I will not." Clea finally managed a thin smile then directed them back to business. "Vora has already turned over evidence about our opponents, all her research data which led her to that dangerous turn of heart. The data has been backed up and secured. The other technicians are being questioned but so far it looks like none of them had anything to do with my...with the traitor."

"Understood." Gray nodded. "What's your assessment of the Crystal Font? Do you think they were destroyed?"

"Personally, I don't believe it," Clea replied. "And I'm not just wishful thinking. Kale proved to be a solid, intelligent officer. I'm certain he thought of something…that he escaped."

"I hope you're right."

"After this mission, I'm willing to go on some faith." Clea settled into her chair and relaxed. "The ground mission pushed me farther than I thought possible. Not only physically either. Those marines are amazing and I feel they are dramatically underestimated."

"Often. Most individual soldiers are. Their feats are pretty incredible and only a few of them were even hurt."

"Cuts, bruises, a couple of minor fractures but otherwise, they returned unscathed. Captain Hoffner picked the right men for the job."

"That's why he's here." Gray sipped again. "I suppose you'll get your promotion now."

Clea nodded, looking down at her hands. "Before, when we were about to leave we talked about the type of officer I've become."

"I remember."

"I feel much more confident. Not only in my abilities but my decision making...my ability to work with others and inspire them. I've learned a lot from you, but quite a bit from Captain Hoffner as well. I saw him do things which astounded me...feats of heroics for his people. He was the last one off the planet and the the first to dive into action. I admire him a great deal."

"There are few finer people to look up to," Gray said. "I've always liked William. He's a straight shooter who tells you what he's thinking. It's one of the reasons I was okay with you hitting the surface with them. I knew you'd be in a good hands."

"I appreciate it. So when I receive my promotion, I will take it with honor now...and not doubt."

"I'll congratulate you when you've got it." Gray took a deep breath. "We've got a long road ahead, don't we?"

"Yes, sir." Clea nodded. "I'm afraid we do. The enemy closes in, they've proven to be far more frightening than we thought and now, our one advantage has been nullified. We return home with more of a disadvantage than when we started but I will not give up hope. Our cultures will band together and fight. None of us will go gentle into that good night."

"Poetry, Clea?" Gray raised his brows. "I'm impressed."

"I like the work of Dylan Thomas," Clea replied. "His words spoke to me. Especially that piece."

"It does have a certain context in our situation, doesn't it?"

Clea frowned, nodding her head once. "It does indeed."

"Shall we pass the time with something less harsh?" Gray motioned to their chess board. "A game before sleep?"

"I'd like that," Clea replied, scooting forward in her seat. "Perhaps exhaustion will give you the advantage you need to defeat me."

"We'll see, Clea." Gray laughed and sipped his drink. "We'll see."

Made in the USA
San Bernardino, CA
20 February 2017